FALLING FOR YOU

BAILEY BLACK

A Note to Readers

This novel was previously published under the pen name Chrissy Brown as Can't Let Go. I struggled with dropping the name because it was my first writing experience. That being said, I'd never felt happy with the original story. So, after much thought, I decided to dive back in. While some parts have stayed the same, it is a completely different story, hence the name change.

Fun fact: the "I'm a bull rider" scene really happened. That's how I met my husband waaay back in the day when I was nineteen. Another fun fact. That's the only part of my life that's in here. All other people, places, and situations are strictly fiction and any resemblances are coincidental.

So, without further adieu, I give you, Josh and Layla.

A chill slithered through me as I looked out the window from my seat in row 23A. Our pilot circled the runway, waiting for the go-ahead from the control tower to launch us into the sky. Tonight's flight would be relatively short, but as my luck would have it, this was an older plane and I couldn't watch a movie.

Adding insult to injury, cellular service was nonexistent while in the clouds, which meant the new books I wanted to read on my Kindle app were useless. I should have downloaded them before takeoff or bought a magazine at the kiosk, but because of my lack of planning, I was stuck on an almost two-hour flight with nothing but my thoughts.

One thought in particular wouldn't leave me alone: *Why was I going back?*

It wasn't the quietness of a small town or how the stars shine brighter away from the big city that drew me in. Nor was my return for the *friends* I left because Hattie Reynolds was the only person to text me since I left.

No, what drew me back to Sebastian Florida was what had kept me away for so long—Joshua Thomas—and it wasn't a matter of *if* I'd run into him; it was when, because Hattie's boyfriend, Landon Waters, was one of Josh's best friends.

I wrapped my arms around my waist and hugged myself. As much as I tried to prepare myself for running into Josh, I wasn't ready to see him again. He broke my heart and I hadn't fully recovered.

Hattie's asked me a hundred times if I still love Josh, and I'd dodged the question more often than not because I wasn't sure.

Love was a fickle word with expectations and the possibility of a future attached to it. Josh and I were never supposed to have a future. I knew that from day one, but I'd never felt a pull to be near someone like I did when I was with him. And a part of me I didn't realize existed shattered when we broke up.

So, that brought me back to my original question. Why come back? Why subject myself to the pain and the embarrassment of looking like an idiot to him and the people I thought were my friends?

The easy answer? Because I was a fool.

What was it Elvis said? Only fools fell in love? Or perhaps it was that they rushed in? I didn't know. However the saying went, I did both—rushed into a relationship and fell too hard.

I slid the window shade up and noticed our pilot circling the landing strip. I'd done it again, gotten lost in my thoughts while time raced away from me. I'd been doing that a lot since moving back to Georgia. Losing time.

Fifteen minutes later, the plane touched down and I was allowed to disembark. I grabbed my rolling carry-on bag and my backpack from the overhead compartment, then shuffled my way through the sea of bodies in the terminal.

After a quick chat with the car rental company and a nerve-racking two-hour drive, I finally made it to the yellow one-bedroom cottage that Hattie and Landon called home. No one paid me any attention as I crossed the grassy knoll beside the house, a cruel reminder that these people were never really my friends.

The front door was open, like it was more often than not. I took a deep breath, hoping it would settle my nerves, and headed toward the kitchen. Tonight wasn't a night I wanted to tackle sober.

I opened the fridge and grabbed a plastic container filled with what I hoped was watermelon-flavored Jello. I swiped my tongue around the inside edge, loosening the gelatinous goo, and swallowed. Without giving myself time to change my mind, I grabbed a beer—even though I had never been a fan—and took a big guzzle of that, too. I wanted the alcohol to bury my fear and anxiety, but most importantly, I needed it to put a blindfold over my heart.

"Ahhhhh!" a girl screamed from behind me and I recognized the high-pitched squeal.

Hattie ran into the kitchen, hands waving about like a madwoman, before throwing them around my neck. I peeled her blue-tinged strands from my lipstick and forced a laugh as we stumbled back and into the fridge. I was happy to see Hattie, and for someone to be excited I was here, but I didn't feel gleeful. My skin crawled, my stomach twisted, and I needed her to let me go before I hyperventilated. "Good to see you too, Hattie."

"You have no idea how much I've missed you." She released me just as the world began to spin out of focus.

I bit my lip, wondering if I should have waited until morning to come by. I could have blamed missing her nineteenth birthday on a delayed flight, or even traffic, but I knew if I didn't come out tonight I wouldn't have shown up at all.

Hattie grabbed my hand and dragged me across the tiny kitchen to the living room. "Two months is too long and Savannah is too far away. I thought having you in Orlando was rough, but at least I saw you on the weekends. What do I have to do to get you to move back to Florida? I miss my best friend."

My gaze bounced around her tiny apartment as memories clouded my thoughts. I'd spent so much of the last year in this house, with Hattie and her friend group, that even the memories that shouldn't hurt still cut deep. "I missed you too, but I don't know if I can come back. It's up to my guidance counselor."

"That's so lame." She dropped her head back dramatically, then started to fill me in on everything I'd missed the past two weeks, which was mostly drama related to Kelly.

I looked around the tiny room again, unable to shake the heaviness in my chest. Nothing had physically changed; everything was the same as it was eight weeks ago, but there was a shift.

Maybe it was me.

Maybe I was different.

1 year earlier

A dark-haired girl in faded skinny jeans and a floral crop top leaned against an older-style red Nissan Altima, probably waiting for me. She popped her gum, not bothering to glance up from her phone as my rental car's headlights painted her yellow.

I parked behind the Nissan and pressed the lock button on my key fob out of habit. This neighborhood seemed safe enough with its picket fences and solar-powered street lights, but at this point, clicking the button again to unlock it was redundant.

"I take it you're Layla?" the girl was supposed to babysit asked.

I smiled and tried to look excited about tonight. If I did my job right, the night would end with Killy thinking her mom and my aunt set us up on a blind friend date because I was visiting from Savannah.

She doesn't need to know that I'd been sent as insurance. If Kelly stayed out of trouble, her mom promised to donate to my Aunt Tricia's latest fundraiser.

I didn't know what made tonight so special, but my job was to make sure Kelly didn't get arrested, pregnant, or do anything to jeopardize the twenty-thousand-dollar check coming our way on Sunday.

But hanging out with strangers for the night, doing god-knows-what, was one hundred percent out of my comfort zone. I was an introvert at heart, only going out when absolutely necessary, and this was my personal hell.

"You must be Kelly." I extend my hand and let it hang in the air for a solid three seconds before dropping it back to my side.

Kelly rolled her eyes and turned around while unlocking her car. "Let's go."

I pat my back pockets, double-checking that I grabbed my phone because it held my life—my driver's license and my debit card. Satisfied I wasn't leaving anything behind, I had no choice but to join her in the little Nissan.

Kelly's door creaked as it opened. I forced another smile, even though the woman barely glanced at me, just in case she was embarrassed that her front seat was disgusting. The floor-board and seat were covered in receipts, fast food bags—that I hope were empty—and gas station Slurpee cups. I pushed everything in the seat onto the floorboard, listening to the crunch under my feet, then buckled up.

Going solely off what my Aunt Tricia told me about Kelly—that her parents thought she parties too much and might've needed rehab—I figured we were going to a party. I just hoped tonight wouldn't be as much of a disaster as her car was.

Kelly turned her key in the ignition, then faced me and wrinkled her nose. "Are you going to church?"

I tug the ends of the three-quarter sleeve pink sweater covering my black tank top. I paired it with a pair of dark skinny jeans and ankle-high boots—something my mother would have skinned me alive for if work to church. "No."

"Coulda fooled me," Kelly scoffed, rolling her eyes again. She shifted the car into gear but hesitated before pulling out of her driveway. "Just so we're clear if anyone asks, I don't know you."

"Got it." I tucked my lips between my teeth and nodded, slightly relieved. Judging by the leather miniskirt and neon orange tube top Kelly wore, I'd figured she was the kind of girl who craved attention. I could've been wrong, but we'd see.

Me, I was the blend-into-the-background kind of girl. Pretending not to know Kelly unless in the confines of her car was fine be me.

~

THREE PARTIES, one McDonald's drive-through run, a quick stop on the side of the road to pee, and we were finally headed back to Kelly's house.

I was beyond ready. Back home, I went out every now and then when my parents forced me to, but I'd never willingly stayed out this late.

"I take it you lost that last round of beer pong?" I asked when Kelly gave up singing Katy Perry's *I Kissed A Girl* to plant a wet one on my cheek.

"I haven't won a game of beer pong since I was sixteen." Kelly threw her head between her legs and tossed one empty McDonald's cup after another behind her into the back seat. She sat up, her head finding the headrest with a thud and groaned. "I think I lost my phone."

I pressed my lips into a line and fought a scowl. Kelly was a train wreck of epic proportions. Her flip-flop broke two parties ago, she'd slept with three guys that I know of, and now she couldn't remember where she'd tucked her phone.

Do I think she needed rehab?

No, but if you looked up *hot mess* in the dictionary, you'd find her picture instead of a definition.

"It's in your bra."

"Huh?" Kelly looked down, finally realizing the end of her

bright pink iPhone case was visible between her massive chest and orange top. She squealed, then laughed. "There it is!"

My aunt sure knows how to pick them.

"Hey, I know that truck!" Kelly pulled her phone from her shirt and squinted at its backlight, somehow managing to find the number she was looking for. "Hey, sexy thing. What are you doing?"

Her high-pitched voice faltered when the mystery man on the other end talked. I couldn't understand what he was saying, but I knew what he wanted. By the way Kelly licked her lips, it seemed like she was ready for round four. She hung up and said, "Turn there."

"No. It's like two in the morning. I need to get you home so I can drive back to Orlando and go to bed."

"It's too late to drive back to your aunt's place. Just crash at my house tonight." Kelly folded her hands, prayer style, and begged, "Please."

Considering I had to go back to her house for my rental car anyway, staying with Kelly tonight didn't sound like the worst idea. At least there I could sleep in. Aunt Tricia insisted the whole house be up at five a.m., no matter what day of the week it was. "Fine."

Kelly shrieked and pointed at an upcoming streetlight. "There! Turn there!"

After more wrong turns than right, we eventually made it to an empty church parking lot, seconds before a truck pulled in. Kelly jumped out of the passenger seat before I could shift her car into park.

I watched her wait like a kid on Christmas for her newest conquest: a lanky blonde who was attractive but not my type.

The guy held his arms out, and Kelly ran into them, jumping and latching her legs around his waist. He fused his mouth to hers, carried her back to his truck, and lowered the tailgate.

I leaned the seat of the Nissan back and closed my eyes. The last thing I wanted to see was someone's white ass in the air... or any other body parts.

The car door opened again and I squeezed my lids tighter, casting out the overhead light's brightness. I sensed a body next to me, but it didn't smell like Kelly. It smelt like whiskey, spices, and wood.

Peeling one eye open, I squinted at the intruder. A black cowboy hat shadowed most of the face that was looking at me, but the parts of him I could see were attractive. Strong arms. A tight button-down shirt. And a pair of jeans that didn't leave much to the imagination.

I opened both eyes and lifted my head off the seat. The guy tipped the front of his hat at me. I blushed, not because I was flattered, but because people didn't do things like that where I was from.

"Hey there." He had a thick, southern accent, too strong for a Florida boy. I fought a smile as I sat my seat up. The passenger door closed and the overhead light went out almost immediately, but the streetlamp's glow was bright enough that I could somewhat make out his face. He leaned forward, turned the music down, and said, "You're pretty."

I couldn't tell if the over-annunciation was from that southern twang or if it was alcohol-induced. Either way, this guy's accent was sexy. I felt his eyes on me, waiting for the acknowledgment I refused to give. I watched Mr. Cowboy shift from the corner of my eye. He leaned forward and rested his elbows on his knees, hands clasped together.

What is he doing?

He sat up straight and leaned closer until his warm whiskey breath tickled my cheeks. Heat climbed my neck at the thought of him kissing me. Not because I was interested—I wasn't—but I'd only kissed one man: my ex, Ashley.

"I'm a bull rider."

I laughed and the guy's head cocked to the side. He didn't honestly expect that line to work. Did he?

What tiny butterflies I may have felt about Mr. Cowboy kissing me disappeared. Kelly needed to hurry up and finish because I wanted to get as far away from this loser as possible.

Kelly was on Sam like white on rice before I could make it around the front of my truck. Sam would have fucked her right there in the parking lot, but that wasn't cool. Kelly may have been easy, but she still deserved some semblance of privacy.

"Y'all wanna use my—"

They climbed into the back before I could finish getting the words out. Shaking my head, I made my way over to Kelly's car. Knowing her, she left it unlocked and running for a quick get-in-get-out kind of thing.

Opening the passenger door, I had every intention of laying the seat back and closing my eyes. This wasn't my first rodeo with those two; this little sexcapade could last a while.

The overhead light clicked on when the door opened, and my breath caught in my chest. The most beautiful girl I'd ever seen was sleeping in the driver's seat. Something inside of me shifted. The need to talk to this girl and make a good impression consumed me. She opened one eye and looked up. Realizing the light must have woken her, I tipped my hat and slipped in the passenger seat so the light could click off.

"Hey there." Fucking, hell. What was I, sixty? Who talked like this? Why couldn't I be normal and just say *hi*?

The girl didn't say anything. She didn't smile, but her gaze darted over to me a few times. *Maybe I can save this.* "You're pretty."

"Thanks." She looked out the window toward my truck.

I stared at her, waiting for her to look at me again. One second. Two seconds. Four seconds. *Shit.*

There was no other choice. I had to pull out my go-to line. It was a hook, line, and sinker every time. "I'm a bull rider."

It all started with her eyes. They found me first and then her head turned. A fraction of a second later, the corners of her mouth lifted into a small but noticeable smirk.

There was a sweet satisfaction knowing that I'd broken through her façade, but all I wanted was to taste those lips. I'd probably be useless for anything else tonight. *Gotta love Jack Daniels.*

I leaned closer and her scent made my head swim. Flashing my best smile, I said again, "I'm a bull rider."

The girl laughed and shook her head. I might've been offended if I hadn't drank a fifth of whiskey, but I found her resistance endearing. Most of the girls around here threw themselves at me, but not this one. The fact that she didn't want me made me want her even more. One way or another, I would win her over.

She turned her head, bringing her gaze to mine. It was too dark to tell what color her eyes were, but I bet they were beautiful. "I have a boyfriend."

"I don't see him here tonight." I reached my hand out and touched her cheek. I stared at her lips, unable to think about anything else. Most of the girls I screwed around with tasted like beer. I'd put money on it that this one didn't. I was guessing she'd taste like cherry because of the Chapstick in the center console.

The overhead light clicked on, blinding me. My eyes were slow to adjust, but when they did, I opened the passenger door, stood, and watched this chick cross the parking lot.

She pounded her fist against the side of my truck, a move that would have gotten her face beaten if she were a dude. "I swear to god, Kelly, if you aren't in your car in one minute, I'm leaving without you."

"**G**et up, bitch, we're going to the beach."

I groaned and pulled the blanket over my head. My whole body ached and I didn't have one drop of alcohol last night.

I was an eight-hours-of-sleep kind of girl, and judging by how shitty I felt, I'd say I got five at best. How Kelly was functioning at full speed after getting rip-roaring drunk was beyond me. My blanket was ripped from my body, and I was forced to open my eyes.

"You can borrow this." Kelly tossed a bikini at my feet, then turned back to the mirror on her dresser and continued to line her eyes.

I picked up the hot pink strings and wondered how these scraps covered anything. I'd worn bikinis before. I had an entire drawer back home, but they all had more fabric than this.

"I should get going. My Aunt Tricia is probably wondering where I am."

"She's not." Kelly capped her eye pencil and opened a tube of mascara. "Mom said you were staying with us until tomorrow. I figure if I've got to babysit you, the least we can do is get you in the sun so you don't look like you crawled out of a coffin for tonight's party."

My jaw dropped at the thought of spending the weekend with Kelly. I shoved my hand under the pillow and searched for my phone. When I found it, there was an unread message from my aunt.

AT: Status update.

"I...um...I'm going to step outside and make a quick phone call."

Kelly didn't acknowledge me as I walked out of her room. I paused in the hallway and looked around. Her house was designed where a living room/dining room combo separated the master bedroom from the other two rooms. I unlocked her sliding glass door, and the moment her three Yorkies heard that click, they were at my feet, ready to go out.

"Sorry, little guys." I pushed them back, then closed the slider. I didn't want to be responsible for losing her dogs or, better yet, have to run this early in the morning because they escaped.

Sitting in one of the plastic chairs, I opened my recent calls and clicked *AT*. It rang twice before she answered, "How was last night?"

"Good, I guess. No one got arrested and I'm pretty sure Kelly isn't pregnant."

Talking to Aunt Tricia had always been awkward. Be it by FaceTime or voice calls, our conversations were filled with long pauses and curt answers. It was part of the reason I preferred to text, but Aunt Tricia was old school. Even if the conversation only lasted a minute or two, she was a 'hear your voice' kind of person.

"Keep it that way until after the fundraiser tomorrow and we'll be set."

I didn't expect words of praise from my aunt, but they would have been nice to hear. So would a warning that I was expected to stay the weekend in this podunk town. "About that. Kelly said I'm staying the night again?"

"Don't be such a child, Layla," my aunt scolded.

I heard her morning mimosa clank against the sunroom's glass table. I was surprised she wasn't at work yet. With the teen shelter fundraiser tomorrow, she should have been at the venue overseeing the setup and confirming the final menu with the caterers. I looked at the phone, noting it's already nine. *Odd.*

"I just—"

Click.

Aunt Tricia hung up, not caring enough to hear how I would have been of better use in Orlando, helping to put the finishing touches on my first-ever fundraiser before heading back home. Instead, I was stuck in the tiny town of Sebastian with a chick I didn't know, no clothes of my own, and a dying phone.

The patio door slid open. Kelly poked her head out and scowled. "You're not dressed yet?"

She rolled her eyes and slipped back into the house. I took a deep breath and ran my hands through my hair. This was going to be a long weekend.

I hid under the shade of Kelly's pink and white Walmart umbrella. My skin hurt—physically hurt—because we'd been sitting on the beach for hours, and there were parts of me that were seeing the sun for the first time.

Ever.

We didn't have beaches where I lived, just large lakes surrounded by grass and cream-colored dirt. I had a pool in my backyard, but it was nothing compared to this. The sand down here was a blinding white, reflecting the sun's rays, essentially turning the world into an oven and me into its roast.

"Can we leave yet?" I touched my arm and winced. A white circle appeared and then disappeared on my rose-colored skin. I'd passed tan an hour ago and had gone full-blown lobster. "I think I'm burning."

"Seriously?" Kelly tilted her sunglasses so I could see her brown eyes roll. I didn't think she wanted me here any more than I wanted to be. "Don't you know anything? Beaches are an all-day thing. Besides, I need at least another forty-five minutes to keep my skin's golden glow."

I groaned and grabbed a water bottle from her cooler bag, crossing my legs and trying to hide in as much of the shade as possible. Unlike Kelly, who seemed to turn shades of brown instead of red, too much more of this and I was going to look like an onion: a peeling mess—the perfect souvenir from Florida.

Kelly's phone dinged. She rolled onto her side to read the message, smiled briefly, then said, "We have company."

I looked up and noticed a group of people walking toward us, one girl seemingly leading three guys. Kelly climbed to her feet and brushed the sand off her ass. She emitted a high-pitched squeal that made me cringe, then ran toward the girl in a flowing white dress.

Kelly wrapped her arms around the girl's neck until a tattooed guy said something. I couldn't hear what it was, but she flipped him the middle finger in response. They walked over to our spot, and Kelly resumed her place on her towel again. "So, guys, this is Layla. Mom says I have to babysit her this weekend."

I bit my tongue and forced myself to smile. If anyone needed a babysitter around here, it was Kelly. She was about as responsible as a six-year-old in a candy store with a pocket full of cash before dinner.

The girl in the white dress dropped her aqua 'Be a Mermaid and Make Waves' beach bag and extended her hand. "I'm Hattie."

"Layla."

"Like the song by Eric Clapton?" The tattooed guy, who had aggravated Kelly, handed a dark-haired guy an umbrella. That one refused to look at me, focusing all his attention on burying the metal post in the sand. I nodded, and the tattooed one added, "Cool. I'm Landon."

"It's a good song," a blonde guy said. He looked vaguely familiar, and I wondered if he had been at one of the parties Kelly had dragged me to last night. "I'm Sam, and this fucker over here is Josh."

Sam hooked his arm around Josh's neck and rubbed his fist into Josh's dark hair like he would if Josh were an eight-year-old kid. They wrestled, like brothers do, until they fell to the sand. Sam released Josh, and they laughed as if this was an everyday occurrence.

I took in each guy as they arranged themselves on the sand. All of them were beautiful, but Josh drew my attention the most. Sure, he was handsome in that classic boy-next-door kind of way, with his dark brown hair and caramel-colored eyes, but there was something about him that I couldn't put my finger on. Sam might have looked like someone I'd met before, but Josh felt familiar.

Sam laid his towel beside mine, which earned me a scowl from Kelly, but I couldn't have cared less. I wasn't interested in someone who was probably sloppy seconds. "So, what brings you to our neck of the woods?"

I didn't make a habit of telling people that my aunt was Tricia Collins. Her name carried weight in the right circles, and while I doubted anyone here knew who she was, I'd rather not earn favoritism or criticism from association. "I'm visiting from Georgia to work at a nonprofit organization with my aunt."

Not a lie. Just not the whole truth. Besides, the chances of running into any of these people beyond this weekend were slim to none.

"That's a horrible way to spend Spring Break. What are you, thirty?" Kelly grumbled. She rolled onto her back and threw her arm over her eyes. I hoped she got a white tan line across her face.

"Ignore her." Hattie laid a giant blanket before me and then rolled onto her belly.

The tattooed guy, Landon, slapped her ass. She narrowed her eyes at him, then giggled. Josh had taken a seat in the furthest shaded spot away from me. I gazed at the horizon, unsure of what else to say. No one was asking me questions, and I wasn't about to voluntarily spill my guts.

"Dude." Landon reached into his cooler and threw a chunk of ice at Josh. "Stop staring, you'll scare her away."

Hattie backhanded Landon across the chest. He gave her a look, then added, "I'm just saying, he looks like a creeper."

Hattie groaned, then rolled into a seated position and twisted the cap off her water bottle. "Ignore him." She took a sip and then set it in the sand beside her. "In fact, ignore all of them. They're nothing but a bunch of idiots." She climbed to her feet and pulled her dress off, revealing a teal cutout one-piece. "Come on, let's go swimming."

The thought of exposing myself to the sun any more than I already had made my stomach twist. Adding third-degree burns because I was trying to keep up with people I didn't care about did not sound like my idea of fun.

Nevertheless, I put my best face forward and pretended to be excited that I was invited while feeling remorseful to decline. I probably would have said yes if they had been here an hour ago. Hattie seemed nice, and so did Landon and Sam. The jury was still out on Josh. "I think I'll stay here."

Hattie smiled in acknowledgment and strode toward the shore with Landon close behind. The moment Sam climbed to his feet, Kelly was up and chasing after him, which left Josh and me alone, and for some reason, that made me nervous.

"Your shoulders are red." Josh pointed at my angry skin.

My shoulders, arms, neck, and back were also burnt. The spaghetti-strap dress Kelly had loaned me didn't help the situation either.

Josh shrugged his yellow short-sleeve tee off and held it out to me. "Here, I doubt it'll keep you from peeling, but it should help."

"Thanks." I slipped the shirt over my head and fought a grimace as it touched my skin.

When my brother, Colson, gave me his shirt—or any of his friends, for that matter—it was tossed at me like I was a nuisance. Josh acted like giving me the shirt off his back was second nature. Maybe that was why I didn't feel weird sniffing it as it slipped past my nose and onto my shoulders.

"I'm sorry about last night." He leaned over the edge of the blanket and grabbed a handful of sand, then sifted the grains through his fingers, building a tiny collapsing castle by his feet.

"I don't know what you're apologizing for," I told him honestly.

Josh smirked, his shoulders lifting with a tiny laugh as he met my gaze. I liked his eyes. At first glance, they were nothing more than brown, but when you looked closely, they were the color of honey with gold swirls and, in the right light, some green pigmentation.

"You had that many drunk guys hitting on you last night?"

I didn't know whether to be flattered that Josh thought I had garnered that much attention or offended. My jaw fell open, and I wasn't sure how to respond. I mean, I had a handful of guys flirt with me, but I thought they assumed I was promiscuous, like Kelly. Once I threw it out there that I had a boyfriend and wouldn't be indulging in their fantasies, they all backed off.

All but one.

"It's okay," he continued. "I don't blame those guys. You're beautiful, but for the record, I was the babbling idiot who made a fool of himself in the church parking lot last night."

"Oh," I said, finally realizing how I knew him and Sam. "You were there when Kelly and Sam... you know."

Josh laughed again, and this time it was a little lighter. The sound made me grin and his smirk stretched wider. Josh had a nice smile accented by his jawline. "Yeah, Kelly and Sam have an on-again, off-again, open relationship of sorts. Sam likes to keep things open."

"Like her legs?" I covered my hand with my mouth, not meaning to have said that out loud. "Oh. My. Gosh."

"Don't feel too bad, you're not wrong." Josh guffawed. "There's a reason why I've never touched Kelly like that and never will."

Knowing that he'd never hooked up with Kelly was oddly satisfying. We could never be a thing. I lived too far away, and we had just met, but still. If the sun and moon aligned and the opportunity presented itself, I wasn't sure I could be with Josh if he had jumped on the Kelly wagon.

"So, how do you all know each other?"

Josh smiled and I noticed he did that a lot. The guy generally seemed happy and not weighed down by the world. All of his friends seemed to have missed the we're-going-to-be-grownups-get-your-life-together memo. Or if they did get it, they were in a place where they didn't care. Either way, I was a little jealous.

"Landon and I have been friends since grade school. Hattie came around when they started dating a few months ago. I didn't like the idea because she's a senior in high school, but her parents are cool with it, so who am I to judge?"

"Is he that much older?" I glanced at the water. Hattie, Landon, Sam, and Kelly were gathered in almost a circle. They were laughing at something Landon had said, oblivious to the fact that we were talking about them. Looking at the group, I never would have guessed Hattie was a year younger than me. She carried herself with confidence. It made her look older.

"Landon failed kindergarten and third grade. So, even though we graduated together a couple of years ago, he's already almost twenty-three."

My dad would have killed me. He'd told me for as long as I could remember that I couldn't date until graduation. I could only imagine how he'd react if I brought home an older, tattooed man when the time came.

"Sam and my brother, Bret, played on the same t-ball team, which is how I got to know him. My uncle used to be a volunteer coach. He knew Sam's home life was rough. I can't begin to tell you how often he forced Sam to come to dinner and stay over. We eventually became friends simply because he was around so much. Now, he's family."

"I have a brother, too." As soon as the words left my mouth, I felt lame. I'd never been good at talking to guys, especially if they were hot, which was why I avoided it most of the time.

I was only dating Ashley because our getting together had practically been arranged at birth. Even so, it didn't make things any less awkward between us.

"My brother, Bret, is two years older than me and studying to be a doctor in Gainesville. He claims he wants to help people, but I know the truth." Josh paused, baiting me into a question.

"And what's that?"

"He wants to flash his doctor status to score that nurse-pussy."

"Oh!" My cheeks heated. Thankfully, they were too burnt for Josh to see how red he'd made me. I was sure Colson and his friends talked like this; they just never did around me. As for my friends, they were a bunch of earth-loving, debate-winning nerds. I was pretty sure they'd self-combust if they replaced the human anatomy with slang words.

Josh grew silent for a few minutes, which was fine by me because he made me nervous in ways I didn't realize were possible. I'd felt my stomach twist when it came to public speaking and had bile climb my throat before a test, but this was different. The knots in my stomach didn't twist; they fluttered, and I couldn't decide if I wanted Josh to go into the water with his friends or stay with me.

"You don't seem to be having too much fun."

I shook my head. "No, the beach isn't really my thing. I have to constantly be doing something or my mind wanders. Sitting still for hours like this is killing me."

Josh nodded in understanding while taking time to choose his words. "I work outside in the heat. It used to be just a few hours here and there, but since I graduated, I have to be there six days a week from dawn until dusk. Weekends are a bit more flexible, but not by much. So, sitting in the sun is not exactly what I call fun either."

I wracked my brain, trying to think of a job that would require a twenty-something-year-old to work such crazy hours.

I had nothing.

After a long stretch of silence, Josh asked, "Do you wanna get out of here?"

"Won't your friends be mad?"

He shook his head and smirked. "If they need to leave—which I doubt, those guys can spend hours here and not bat an eye—everyone can fit in Kelly's car. Besides, they're used to me coming and going randomly. They know my hours are whacked and don't think twice when I disappear."

I sat and thought about Josh's words for a minute. Leaving Kelly might mean I won't get asked to work with my aunt again this summer, but Kelly was at the beach with her friends. Friends that seemed nice. How much trouble could she get into in a group in broad daylight?

I nodded, which earned me another gorgeous smile from Josh. He stood and pointed behind me. "I know a sandwich shop just about a block from here. We can walk there if you're hungry."

"I'm not, but I don't mind going if you are."

The Red Onion had always been a beach staple around here. Sure, there were other sandwich shops on the strip across the street, but not one of them could make a lobster roll like Cooper Harris. That man knew his sandwiches, burgers, and basically everything food-related.

The overhead bell chimed as I opened the door. I held it, letting Layla pass through, then followed behind. She had said she wasn't hungry, but I was hoping I could get her to at least try something.

I had made a horrible first impression last night. Even though I knew I'd eventually get a second chance—small town and all—I hadn't expected it to be so soon, with my last blunder still fresh.

"Joshua Thomas." Cooper extended his hand for our usual fist bump. Before graduation, I had come here at least once a week to grab a bite to eat and chill. Since taking over most of the responsibilities at my paw's ranch, this was my first time making it out this way in weeks. "Long time, man. Where've you been hiding out?"

"With Bret at Gainesville University this past year and Paw's radiation therapy, I had to pick up the slack on the ranch."

Paw owned roughly eighty acres out in West Fellsmere. We used to have more land, but back when he was a boy his parents had to sell some of it.

I was glad.

Eighty acres was already too much for Paw and me to handle, and when Bret left, he had refused to hire a day worker. That had put me between a rock and a hard place, having to choose between my family and college after graduation. There was no choice, not really.

Family came first.

Always.

"That's right. I forgot he left." Cooper flipped his notepad open and grabbed a pen. "Sorry you're stuck, man, but what can I get you?"

"The usual—lobster roll, chips, and a large sweet tea."

Cooper scribbled my order and then looked up. "And for the lady?"

Layla shook her head and smiled politely. Her cheeks flushed red as she said, "Nothing for me, thanks."

"Dude." Cooper dropped his pen, set his palms on the counter, then leaned forward. He was a big guy, standing at almost six-foot-three and built like a brick house. Under the wrong circumstances, Cooper could be scary, but most of the time, he was a giant softie. "Is your girl too good for my food?"

Layla's blue eyes widened. She sucked in an audible breath, the red hue creeping down her neck as she shook her head. "No! Never. I'm just not hungry."

Cooper narrowed his eyes and stared Layla down for a solid three seconds before letting out a boisterous laugh. "Lighten up, sweetheart. I'm kidding."

Layla exhaled, her shoulders rolling forward as she chuckled. It dawned on me that she had been nervous, possibly even scared I'd let someone hurt her. The thought lit me up and made me sick to my stomach at the same time. What kind of jerks had she been hanging out with?

I paid Cooper, then led Layla to a corner table by the window. She took the chair opposite me and smiled nervously. "So."

"So." I tilted my straw in her direction, offering some tea, but she shook her head.

Layla fidgeted with her hands under the table, her nervousness given away by her reflection in the window. I liked that she was nervous. It meant I was having an effect on her, that there might be a chance I could make up for being an ass last night.

"Here." Cooper set a bag of chips before Layla while handing me my basket. "Only a dick makes his date watch him eat."

"You're a jerk," I said at the same time Layla added, "We're just friends."

Chapter 7

I should have been licking my wounds at the blow of being just friends, but I was happy. Last night, I had been nothing more than a horny cowboy. Today, we were friends. In my book, that was progress in leaps and bounds.

I picked up my sandwich and took a bite. It was heaven in my mouth. I didn't know what Mamma T would do when Cooper left for the military next month. He lived and breathed this shop, and the dedication showed in everything Cooper made.

"I'm sorry," Layla said nervously. "Was this supposed to be a date?"

I shook my head and took another bite. "Can't be on a date since you have that boyfriend."

I winked, and Layla's cheeks flushed. She stared at her bag of chips for a few seconds before pulling it apart at the seam. I watched her inspect a chip, taking in every detail as if it were the first time she'd seen one. She put the crispy potato slice in her mouth, closed her eyes, and smiled as she swallowed.

"Good?"

Layla's eyes snapped open. Her cheeks flushed again, and I loved how easy she was to read. She was like an open book. It was refreshing. The girls around here tried to hide what they wanted, playing that mysterious game that was nothing but bullshit. They wanted one thing and one thing only. Sex.

"I...uh...have to go to the bathroom." Layla looked around, a frown falling upon her face. "Is there a bathroom here?"

"Cooper!" I hollered, causing Layla to jump, and I had to hide my smirk. I hadn't meant to scare her, but discovering how easily she turned red was amusing. I might have to make a game out of it and see how often I could make her blush.

He came around the corner, a cocky grin on his face. "You rang, my dear?"

I flipped him the bird while Layla asked, "Is there a bathroom I can use?"

Cooper nodded and pointed to the kitchen entrance behind the counter. "Around the corner. You can't miss it."

Layla followed his directions and disappeared deeper into the shop. Cooper plopped into her chair across from me and shook his head. "I know that look. Don't do it."

"Do what?"

Cooper's smile fell, his face becoming grimly serious. "Fall for a girl who won't love you back."

I laughed because I had no intention of falling in love with Layla No-Last-Name. I just wanted to get to know her and maybe have a little fun before she went back to Georgia. No harm, no foul. Love wasn't even in the same ballgame. "Don't worry, I won't."

Layla came out of the bathroom a few minutes later, a frown tugging at her pretty lips. "My aunt called. I need to get back to Orlando."

"Well, that sucks." A frown of my own tugged at my lips, but I held it back. "Can I take you back to Kelly's house to get your car?"

Layla nodded, and I slid my newly empty food basket toward Cooper, who shot me a sideways glance. The trash can was less than two feet to my right, but he wasn't doing anything at the moment, and I liked giving him a hard time.

I met Layla at the checkout counter and dropped a five-dollar bill in the tip jar. "Later, Cooper."

Layla waved goodbye, and we walked to my truck in silence. Judging by the worry wrinkles taking up residence between her brows, something was weighing heavily on her mind.

"Everything okay?" I asked, opening the passenger door for her.

She looked up at me briefly, smiled, and nodded. I didn't push the subject. Women were like vaults and wouldn't tell you what was wrong until they were ready.

Luke Combs' latest album filled the silence on the ride to Kelly's house. Layla stared out the window, twisting her phone between her fingers until we pulled into Kelly's neighborhood. I parked in the driveway while Layla leaned forward and turned down the radio. "Thank you for today, Josh. I had a great time."

I smiled, oddly happy at the sound of my name rolling off her lips. "Think we can do it again next weekend?"

"I... um." Layla looked down at her hand, squeezing her phone until the whites of her knuckles showed. "I'm going back to Savannah on Monday. Tomorrow is my last day in Florida, and there's this fundraiser I've got to help with, so..."

It felt like the wind had been knocked out of me. I had been hoping for a few weeks to give Layla a reason to talk to me after she left and maybe even come back again. Now, I had only minutes. "Can I call you sometime?"

Layla nodded, and I handed my phone over to her. She typed in her number, then pressed a quick kiss on my cheek. "Bye, Josh."

5 Months Later

"Layla?" someone asks from behind me.

My name didn't immediately register because everyone I'd worked with this summer called me Miss Price. I kepr working, ensuring each item on my clipboard's checklist was completed as I had for every fundraiser since returning to Orlando in May.

My parents hadn't been happy when I broke off my arranged engagement with Ashley, but I couldn't do it. I couldn't commit myself to a life of fake smiles, Prozac, and a loveless relationship. I was nineteen. I wanted to be at college, breaking out of my shell and learning to live on my own.

Our compromise had been that I would spend the summer working for my aunt, and if I could make it without asking for help, Dad would pay for me to go to college. Financially, I had been cut off, with the exception of having a safe place to live, and forced to survive on the sixteen dollars and fifty cents an hour wage I was paid bi-weekly until classes started the following week. Then, I would get a monthly allowance of nine hundred dollars on top of my wages.

It sucked, but struggling to make it on my own this summer was better than settling for a life half-lived.

That day's event room was large, chosen to seat the two hundred guests who had paid a pretty penny for an adequate dinner. After dinner, there would be a silent auction. The socialites my aunt had rounded up would bid on various donated packages, committing themselves to pay a minimum of double the face value.

Why?

So they could feel good about themselves. Money, while a necessary evil in life, corrupted the soul. The people who had it complained about a six-dollar latte but then spent three hundred dollars on a pair of shoes. All the while, the common working class scraped to get by.

And then there was Aunt Tricia, who refused to spend an unnecessary penny, choosing to exist like she was struggling when her friends weren't around but threw money around like it was confetti once she had an audience.

"Layla!" the female voice called again. I scanned the room, quickly finding an excited girl with long blue dreads setting a box of what I assumed were the hors d'oeuvres we had ordered on one of the buffet tables.

"Hattie?" I asked, completely dumbfounded. Of all the people to run into, I had never expected to see anyone from Sebastian. "What are you doing here?"

Hattie finished setting her boxes on the table and strode across the room to me. She held her arms out, pulling me into a tight hug before saying, "I'm delivering food for my dad's catering company. What are you doing here? I thought you were in Georgia."

"I was. I came back a few months ago, after graduation." I hugged the clipboard to my chest, nervous flutters turning into anxious needles. My shift was officially over in thirty minutes. For now, though, I was still on the clock, and Aunt Tricia hated fraternizing during company time. "I live here now and work for my aunt's crowdsourcing company."

"Shut up! Your aunt is Tricia Collins?" Hattie facepalmed

her forehead and looked around as if seeing the room for the first time. "How did I not know that?"

"Why would you? I didn't tell anybody who she was when I was visiting on Spring Break."

"True, but I've pretty much cyber-stalked you on Instagram since you left." She pulled her phone out of her back pocket and showed me my Instagram feed.

I clicked the home button and found her profile. It was filled with pictures of her and Landon, mostly at parties. I handed her phone back quickly. I didn't want her to realize I had been looking for a picture of Josh. "You're 888big-bootyqueen?"

"Do you not look at the people who follow you?" Hattie chuckled and shoved her phone into her back pocket.

I shook my head and checked my watch. We'd been talking for five minutes, and I still had a whole column of things to do on my paper before heading home to get changed.

I had made it a point to attend the functions I wasn't working. Being in a controlled situation had helped ease my social anxiety, breaking me out of my shell a little. Also, I could pick who I sat with, let them guide the conversations, and have the excuse of needing to help if I got overwhelmed. It had been good for me, and I had met some amazing people.

"I can't believe I ran into you," Hattie said, more to herself than to me. "I know it's random, but do you have plans tonight?"

"Oh, um, I've got a few things to finish here." I wiggled my clipboard, hoping Hattie would get the hint that I needed to get back to work. She nodded, smiling, waiting for me to say something more. "I also thought about attending tonight's event."

"Oh." Hattie frowned, pulled a rubber band off her wrist, and then tied up her long blue strands. "That sucks. I was hoping you'd ride back to Vero with me. It's Landon's twenty-fourth birthday. He's been celebrating all week, but the actual party is…" She looked at her watch and chuckled. "Well, now, but the party will last all night. He probably hasn't even noticed I'm not there yet."

"Layla!" my aunt barked, and the muscles in my back tensed. She strolled across the room, head held high, lips pressed tight. "Have you finished that list?"

I clutched the clipboard to my chest again and shook my head. "Not yet, but I'm close."

Aunt Tricia's lips tilted down into a frown. She didn't like leaving things to the last minute. We still had just under an hour until the event started, but she freaked out if things weren't finished at least a half-hour before the start time. "That's not like you, child."

"I'll get it done before I leave, even if it's on my own time."

"Of course you will." Aunt Tricia turned her attention to Hattie. "Who are you?"

"Hattie Reynolds, ma'am." Hattie held out her hand.

Aunt Tricia took it and forced a smile. "Of course you are." She turned back to me and pointed her red-painted nail at my clipboard. "I don't pay you to talk with your friends. Finish that list in the next fifteen minutes, or you're fired."

My fingers tightened around the clipboard and I had to take a deep breath to calm myself. I hadn't worked harder than every employee Aunt Tricia had for less pay, just so she could fire me on a whim. And I damn sure wasn't about to screw up my future a week before my life started. Dad had agreed to pay for two classes, and I had to finish with straight As if I wanted another tuition stipend next semester, but all of that would go down the drain if I got fired that day.

I hated her. I haded the control she had in my life, but all I could say was, "Yes, ma'am."

"Crap," Hattie mumbled with a frown when my aunt left. "I'm sorry."

"It's fine, but I should go." I looked down at the fifteen items left, knowing I could probably finish half the list if I ran, but not all of it. Tears welled in my eyes at the realization that my one chance to prove I deserved to choose how my life should be lived was shot.

"Wait!" Hattie yelled, skipping to be at my side. "Let me help."

"I don't think so," I said, breezing past the tables to double-check that each setting was correct.

"Please. I feel bad. I didn't mean to get you in trouble." Hattie clapped her hands under her chin and gave me the puppy dog eyes.

I sighed, having lost another three minutes and barely completing one task. "Alright." I scribbled four items on the bottom of my paper and tore it off. "These are pretty self-explanatory. We have twelve minutes. Hurry."

Eleven minutes and thirty-two seconds later, the list was complete. Hattie walked around the room one last time, double-checking that all the place settings were straight, while I approached my aunt.

"Delegation." Aunt Tricia smirked and held her hand out for my clipboard. I handed it over, and she glanced at the list, ensuring each item was finished. "You might just make it in this world. Will we be seeing you tonight?"

"Actually..." Hattie stepped up from behind me and linked her arm to mine. "I was hoping to steal Layla away for the weekend."

Aunt Tricia's eye twitched. "Oh?"

Hattie turned her attention to me. "I just did you a solid. The least you can do is come help me celebrate." She clapped her hands together under her chin again, giving me big, pleading eyes.

I looked to Aunt Tricia for guidance. I didn't know how this situation fell into our arrangement. Even though she was my boss, she was also my aunt and my dad's informant. Leaving with Hattie could potentially screw everything up for me, but I wanted to go. I hadn't done anything fun since moving to Orlando back in May.

Aunt Tricia's face softened, and for the first time since I arrived, she didn't look ready to murder everyone in the room. "I think you should go. You've worked hard the past few months and created strong community bonds. One weekend with people your age seems in order."

Hattie squealed and took my hand. "Thanks, Ms. Collins. You're the best."

The air was thick with sex, pot, and sweat as Hattie took my hand and walked us through the front door of her one-bedroom cottage. The party wasn't huge, but there were more people than I was comfortable with inside her tiny home.

A squeal of excitement sounded during the split-second break of music blasting through the surround sound speakers. I cringed, recognizing it as Kelly's voice and drunken greeting. She cut through the crowd and hurled herself into Hattie's arms like they were long-lost lovers reunited after months apart. "Where have you been? I've been calling you all day!"

"I picked up a surprise when I dropped off my catering order tonight." Hattie took a step back and pulled me by the hand from my hiding space behind her. I tripped over my feet, and she giggled, but not in a *laughing-at-me* kind of way. More like a *you're-too-clumsy-for-your-own-good* kind of way.

I smiled and lifted my hand for a little wave. I didn't get the same vibe from Kelly that I did with Hattie. Hattie seemed like one of those love-everyone, mother-hen kind of friends. With Kelly, I got the feeling that if I pulled her into a hug, she might turn feral and claw my eyes out.

Kelly looked like she'd seen a ghost: mouth slack, eyes wide, neon-orange skin a shade closer to natural. The weight of her stare made my skin crawl with nervousness and confirmed my suspicions that a hug would have been a terrible idea.

"You've got to be kidding me," she finally said, dragging her heavily lined gaze back to Hattie. "What is she doing here?"

"Stop being a bitch, Kelly," Hattie demanded in a motherly tone that said the discussion was over. I was here, and there was nothing Kelly or I could do about it. Hattie set her hand on my arm and smiled. "Be right back."

She stepped around Kelly and headed for the back door. I was tempted to follow, but Kelly's narrow-eyed glare kept me in place.

I shifted on my feet, nervous that she would pounce and rip my head off or something. I had never been in a fight and didn't want to explain to Aunt Tricia why I came to work on Monday with cropped hair (because it had been ripped out) and a busted-up face, assuming Hattie would still drive me back to Orlando tomorrow if I got into a fight with her best friend.

Kelly stepped toward me, shoulders back, hands clenched at her sides. The tiny bubbles of nervous energy simmering under my skin exploded into volcano-sized eruptions. My stomach clenched and twisted because all I could think about was how bad this night was about to go and how much trouble I was going to be in tomorrow. Aunt Tricia could send me home, tail tucked between my legs, reassuring my dad that Florida was a terrible idea.

I bit my lip. Tears pooled from a hypothetical conversation that would determine my future in our family. Everything I had fought for this year was about to go down the drain because of some girl I barely knew. I swallowed the lump in my throat and stood at full height. If I was going down, the least I could do was make the story worth telling.

"You're going to ruin everything." Kelly exhaled, shaking her head, her hard exterior dropping along with her expression. I watched her curiously as she turned and stepped toward the kitchen.

When she didn't immediately return, I realized I was alone,

surrounded by too many people I didn't know. My skin heated again and the room suddenly felt too small and hot. I wasn't good at this—being social, making new friends—not that anyone in this room was or would be my friend.

Kelly made her way back to me after being gone for three songs and extended a beer to me. "If you're going to be here, at least pretend to belong."

I took the can and stared at it for a second, then looked at her again, not trusting that she hadn't somehow poisoned it. Girls were evil, especially when they were jealous of you. That was the only reason I could come up with as to why she was so rude. She was jealous. Of what? I had no clue. She didn't know me or that the shiny picture my family painted was tattered and torn. "Thanks."

I hooked my finger underneath the tab and opened the can. I had never been much of a drinker, even when I was forced to mingle. Pepsi was my go-to because I could easily pretend it had rum or something mixed in it. I didn't know how to fake-drink this.

"For goodness' sake," Kelly murmured. "It's just a beer. Drink it. Don't drink it. I don't care. Just stop looking at it like it's a rabid puppy you want to save but are afraid of."

Bringing the can to my lips, I took a sip. It was cold, which felt good considering how hot the room was, but the beer itself tasted horrible. I tried not to grimace, but Kelly must have noticed because she snorted into her hard lemonade. Thankfully, she didn't say anything.

Hattie walked through the door again, laughing and looking over her shoulder. I stepped toward her, ready to ditch Kelly because she wasn't the best company, when I saw him again.

Josh.

He walked into the room and the air changed, sticking in my lungs. The eyes of nearly every girl turned to him, and for good reason. Josh had been attractive in a teenage boy kind of way back in March. Looking at him now, he was all man with hard edges yet soft eyes.

Dark blue Wranglers hugged every inch of his legs, all the way to his yellow and brown cowboy boots. A black button-down shirt splayed across his chest, holding his arms tight while falling loose near his waist, giving him a built but not meaty look. What got me most was that hair. Short on the sides and a curly mess on top, ruffled like he'd just had sex.

Probably because he did.

Josh laughed at something Hattie said, and his whole face lit up. It was the kind of laugh that would have had my mom scheduling her next Botox treatment, full of life and expression.

Some guy lifted his head in a curt nod, one that said, 'Hey bro, she's here with me,' and I noticed a few other guys—the jealous ones—draping their arms over their girlfriends' shoulders. I understood why, Josh had a presence and it commanded the room.

I took a sip of my beer and chased it with another swallow, the taste becoming more tolerable with each sip. My heart thrummed against my chest with a force that vibrated through my body, but at least it was slowing. Pounding aside, it almost felt normal.

I glanced over my almost full can and our eyes locked. From across the room, they looked brown, but Josh's eyes were so much more than they seemed. I'd never forget the vortex of gold and green swirling within them.

Josh's lips lifted, and I felt it for the second time—my world shifting on its axis.

Everyone had a vice.

Landon smoked like a fucking chimney because it helped him function. When he was a kid, his mom tried putting him on meds for ADHD, but instead of slowing his brain to think like ours do, the drugs caused him to hyperfocus. He could be stuck for hours staring at a spec of dirt, deciphering its origin in our universe.

They tried to get the dosage right for years but never could find the right combination. My brother, Bret, offered Landon his first joint in the seventh grade and he's smoked twice a day since. Landon said it helped to slow the world around him while keeping him present. When he was high, he could enjoy life.

Sam, on the other hand, wouldn't touch a drug with a ten-foot pole. His half-sister overdosed on heroin two years ago and it shook him. They weren't close, not like Bret and me growing up, but considering Sam was unwillingly shoved into his dad's life a few years back, those two had the best relationship in that house.

Sam took the edge off with a pack of smokes and enough liquor to drown Aquaman. Before he turned twenty-one, his drinking was manageable. A few beers after work. A bottle of something on the weekend. Everyone knew his ID was fake, but they sold him the alcohol anyway, rarely telling him no.

Maybe it was the fear of getting caught, but Sam never

pushed his luck. He bought what we needed to have a good time, and that was it. Now... now I wish he'd go back to that.

And then there was me. The weekend drinker, occasional smoker, beyond tired motherfucker. I thought last year was rough when I was a part-time day worker for my paw. I had no idea what I was in for. This summer knocked me on my ass and then kicked me back six feet.

Landon took a hit from his joint and then passed it to me. I placed the paper between my lips and inhaled, ready for the smoke to push this week's stress away. I waited all night for it to work its magic, but it seemed like my stress had its claws so deep into my soul that weed couldn't even help. *Figures.*

I exhaled and passed the blunt to Hattie, not that she needed anything else tonight. She was already giggling like a schoolgirl. I forced a smile as she looked over at me. Whatever she said had everyone laughing, so I laughed, too. My friends are great, but they had no idea what I was going through, and they didn't need to know because, as much as they'd try, they couldn't help.

Hattie reached for my hand. I glanced at Landon before letting her take it. Hattie and I were cool despite how much I didn't want her around when they first started dating. We hit that point in our friendship where we hugged every now and then, and I could pick on her without hurting her feelings, but this was new. Landon was either oblivious to Hattie's hand in mine or simply didn't care.

She pulled me through the back door into their tiny one-bedroom cottage. There were just as many people inside as there had been out. The living room/dining room combo was packed. It was like this every weekend. Landon loved having people around. He could care less if they talked to him; he just loved people.

Sam backhanded me across the chest, and I dragged my gaze over to him, the blunt's magic finally taking hold. The weight of this week still held me down, but I didn't care as much, and that was all I asked for. That and to pass out later.

Sam lazily lifted his lips into a grin. "Dibs."

I followed his gaze across the room to a girl trying and failing to hide her face behind her beer. I sucked in a breath, feeling the air reach the back of my lungs for the first time all summer.

The room spun as if I were drunk, but I hadn't had a drop of alcohol yet. Layla had done this to me the last time she was here, shaken my world up without reason, and I had only known her for a day. I didn't believe in love at first sight—movies made that shit up—but I could say I had never wanted someone as much as I had wanted Layla.

Still wanted Layla.

Too bad she made it clear that she didn't want me. I shook my head and shoved Sam playfully. "The only way you'd nail a girl like her is in your dreams."

"We'll see." He smirked.

Shit.

Sam strode across the room and grabbed two beers from a cooler by the television. My heart was in my throat. I couldn't let Layla hook up with him because I didn't share girls. Sam and Landon might not have had a problem with it, but I knew where those dicks had been—specifically Sam's—and I wouldn't go near some of the girls he had hooked up with with a ten-foot pole.

"Hey, cutie," Sam drawled, his signature panty-dropping smirk in play.

Layla looked up from her feet and lifted her lips into a shy smile. "Hi." Her quiet voice was full, like Jennifer Lawrence's: deep but not manly. She took a sip from her can, finding liquid courage, then stood a little straighter. "Cutie? Is that your thing, giving people pet names?"

"Only when they're as pretty as you are."

Fire bubbled in my veins, feeding a monster that wanted to shove Sam away from Layla, but I contained the beast. I would do everything I could to keep them from hooking up tonight, but if he was what she wanted, then so be it.

"Don't let him fool you." I clapped my hand on Sam's shoulder and forced a smile of my own. "He calls everyone 'cutie.'"

"Way to make a girl feel special." Layla twisted and tossed her beer onto the overflowing trash pile. Sam held an extra can out for her. Layla hesitated for a fraction of a second, then took it with a "Thanks."

I ran a hand through my hair and exhaled through my nose. There was a war raging inside me: jealousy, anger, and nervousness were all fighting a losing battle. If you had asked me ten minutes ago about this war, I would have said I didn't have it in me to fight for a girl, and was too tired to care.

Ask me now, and I'd fight until every man who hit on Layla was in the dirt.

I shouldn't have cared what Layla did or who she did it with. I didn't know her. I didn't like her. And yet, I contemplated murdering Sam if he left with her. "I never said you weren't special."

Layla's cheeks flushed, and for the first time tonight, my smile wasn't forced. She popped the tab on her beer and then took a sip. Her brows pulled together with her first swallow. I didn't think she liked the taste, but she kept that to herself.

"So, cutie," Sam mumbled, stepping closer until he was less than three inches away. Layla looked up to meet his gaze. He smiled down at her and twisted a lock of her hair around his finger. "Can you tell me why I've done nothing but dream about you? I haven't gotten a good night's sleep in weeks."

I shook my head and stole Sam's beer from his hand. He didn't notice, much less care. I brought the metal rim to my lips and closed my eyes as I chugged what was left. I couldn't watch what happened next.

"What the fuck?" Sam growled.

His confusion had me snapping my eyes open. I masked my curiosity by crushing the can and then tossing it aside. If Hattie saw me littering in her house, she'd flip, but she'd also understand and expect me to help clean up tomorrow.

Sam ran his hand down his arm, pushing beads of what smelled like beer to the floor. Layla stood frozen, mouth agape. Her dress was soaked on one side, the hem dripping a puddle by her feet.

Kelly smirked and walked away without a word.

Sam let go of his frustrations toward Kelly as quickly as they came. He had this rare gift of letting everything roll off his back. He eyed Layla like she was a rare-cooked ribeye, licking his lips and said, "This is a sign, cutie. That dress has to go."

L ayla looked up at Sam, too shocked to reply, her mouth hanging open. I stepped forward, brushing my arm against Sam's, and undid each button on my shirt. "Here." I draped it over her shoulders, then set my hand on her hip. "Let's find you something dry to wear."

I guided her away from Sam and all the other assholes who had noticed the pink and grey striped bra peeking through her cream-colored dress. Yes, I was one of those assholes, but I had the decency not to stare. One quick glance was all I needed.

I fished my keys out of my pocket and found the one with the purple holder around it. I slid it into the lock, twisted it, and opened the door to Landon's room. For almost everyone here, the bedroom was off-limits, but Sam and I both had a key, just in case. I rarely used mine. Sam, on the other hand, changed the bed sheets almost every weekend.

Layla stepped into the room first. I hit the light switch and shut the door in one move. She spun on her heels, eyes wide.

"Relax." I held my palms up in surrender. I understood how this might look: a strange man unlocked a bedroom and then shut her inside, but my intentions were good. "We're just here to borrow something of Hattie's for you to wear. That's it."

Layla looked down at her beer-soaked dress and huffed out a sad chuckle. "I don't know if you've noticed, but Hattie and I aren't exactly the same size."

I had noticed, but my momma taught me long ago not to discuss a girl's weight. Most girls were insecure about their bodies for one reason or another, even if they were the most beautiful girl in the room. "Hattie is a little bigger than you, yeah."

"A little?" Layla's brows arched.

I walked to the closet and pulled the string for the bulb. Hattie had at least twenty pounds on Layla, but I knew she had a pile of clothes that were too small she refused to get rid of...somewhere.

I rummaged through her pile of jeans, checking each tag until I finally found one three sizes smaller than the rest. I tossed that one over my shoulder and kept hunting. After a few minutes of searching, I hit the jackpot: a stack of pants and a pair of shorts Hattie probably hadn't worn since middle school.

"Here." I set the pile on the bed and tossed the jeans beside them. "Something here should come close to fitting."

Layla walked to the furthest edge of the bed, putting as much space between us as she could. "You don't think she'll mind?"

I shook my head and stepped back. Hands in my pockets, I leaned against the windowsill. "Nah. I doubt she'll even notice any of this is missing. You can keep my shirt if you'd like. Landon has at least five of mine in the closet."

"Thanks." She picked up a pair of shorts, looked at them, and then set them back on the bed before choosing the jeans. "Is that a bathroom?"

"Yup. You can take a shower, too, if you want, to wash the beer smell off. I'll make sure no one bothers you."

"Okay."

Layla walked across the tiny room to the even smaller bathroom and then shut the door. I didn't move until I heard the faint click of the lock. As I folded Hattie's stuff again, the shower turned on. Water whistled in the pipes, but I doubted anyone could hear it over the music.

After putting Hattie's clothes back at the top of her closet and grabbing a shirt for myself off a hanger, I sat on her bed. Don't ask me how, but she and Landon shared a twin-sized mattress. I could barely fit on a twin by myself, but somehow they slept together on it more nights than not.

My phone vibrated in my jeans for the umpteenth time tonight and as much as I didn't want to, I pulled it from my pocket. Eighteen text messages—all from the same person— would go unanswered until tomorrow. I hit the side button to turn off the screen, but another text came through.

> Amanda: This is bullshit, Josh, and you know it.

"You're still here."

I looked up at the sound of Layla's voice and smiled. Hattie's pants were loose in the legs and hanging on by a thread at Layla's hips. They were obviously too big, but considering her other options, things could have been worse. But what got my lips lifting and heart pounding was that Layla was still wearing my shirt, and it was sexy as hell.

I slid to the edge of the bed and slipped my phone back into my pocket. "Of course. Wouldn't want anyone barging in on you."

Layla chewed on her bottom lip and stared at me. "You're not the same asshole cowboy I remember."

"No, ma'am, I'm not." I chuckled. There was barely a shred of that kid left inside me. This year had beaten him down, kicked him around, and spit on his face. If my life was a game of Jenga, I was one wrong move from everything crashing down.

"Good." She smirked and closed the bathroom door behind her. "I didn't trust him."

"He was a jerk. I wouldn't have trusted him either." I flashed her a grin, then took the ten steps from the bed to the door and reached for the knob. Pulling it open, music seeped into the room. The pounding of the bass vibrated through me. I missed the quietness of Landon's almost soundproof room. Loud noises made me anxious, which was why I used to drink so much. Nowadays, I tried to stay outside where the music was barely more than a quiet hum.

"Wow, that's loud!" Layla yelled. She marched through the living room and wiggled through a crowd. I followed her.

Sam was nowhere to be seen, but that didn't mean Layla wasn't drawing the attention of wandering eyes. I stepped closer and shot a back-off glare at anyone who stared too long.

We stepped out onto the front porch, closed the door behind us, and she sighed. "That's better."

Laughter carried from the backyard. I looked over at the sound and made out the shape of five people standing around a small fire. Silhouettes moved in the dark behind them, some dancing to the hum vibrating through the walls. Others just chilling. I didn't want to go over there. I didn't want to smile, socialize, and pretend that life was great. It wasn't. But I didn't want to leave Layla either. "Do you want a drink or something?"

"We have to go back inside for that, don't we?"

"My truck is over there. I've got a bottle of whiskey in my cooler." I pointed across the grassy knoll towards the Baptist church. I took my usual spot under street light number three, the last paved spot in their lot.

"Is that the same church where Sam and Kelly hooked up?"

"Yeah..." I rubbed at the back of my neck. Suggesting we go to my truck might have been a bad idea. I may have just shot myself in the foot.

Layla looked up at the stars. Her hair fell further down her back, leaving a wet trail everywhere it touched. After a moment of silence, she met my gaze again. This time, I got a good look at her eyes. I thought they were blue last year, but they seemed almost white tonight.

"I've never drank whiskey before. Is it good?"

The night was warm, but a cool breeze sent a chill down my spine, causing goosebumps to break out across my flesh. I rubbed my hands against my arms and Josh noticed. He draped his arm around me and pulled me close, his body a furnace against mine. All too quickly, I was hot.

Too hot.

Unreasonably hot.

The kind of hot that made you sweat, and being this close, I didn't want him to think I smelled bad.

Josh's truck was at the end of the vacant lot, almost to the church. As soon as we were close, he let me go. The air between our bodies was cold, but I was grateful to cool off. I stepped closer to the truck, leaned against the driver's side door, and looked up at the sky.

I had thought the stars were noticeable at my aunt's house, but here, millions of fireballs burned bright, highlighting deep purple shadows in the clouds. Back home, the city lights created a smog-like filter. Even on our clearest nights the sky never looked like this.

I turned my head at the sound of metal scraping against metal. Josh tossed a boot from inside his toolbox to the bed of his truck. Something else clunked—a tool, maybe. After a few minutes of searching, he found what he was looking for and slammed his toolbox shut. I watched him walk around to the tailgate and lower it. He rummaged through his cooler and then sat on his newly made bench.

"You coming?"

I didn't know how I felt hanging out with Josh. People showed their true colors when they were drunk or angry. The Josh I met back in March was a drunk, arrogant jerk. Sure, he made nice at the beach, but I was pretty sure he was trying to save face that day.

He texted me a few times after I left and called once, too, but I never answered. I didn't see the point. When I got back home after Spring Break, my aunt made it clear that my internship hadn't worked out and that I would not be welcomed back. I thought there was no point in making friends I'd never see.

If only I had known.

I eyed the half-empty bottle of whiskey beside Josh, not looking forward to shots. The only time I'd taken shots was at my brother's twenty-first birthday and I was sick for two days after. I swallowed the lump in my throat, hoping that whiskey wouldn't be as cruel to me as the vodka had been.

Josh twisted the cap and put the bottle to his lips. There was an open soda beside him, but he didn't touch it. I wondered if that was for me, but didn't ask.

After his swallow, he held the bottle out. Shutting my eyes, I pressed it to my lips and tipped it back. The bitter flavor was stronger than I liked. I fought the urge to spit it out and swallowed with a grimace. He chuckled and held the soda out to me. I traded him and pushed the fire further down my throat.

"You're brave. Most girls would have complained about the afterbite." Josh tipped back the bottle and took a gallon-sized swallow, as if it didn't singe his insides.

"Good thing I'm not like most girls." Our eyes locked, and something passed between us.

Josh gripped my hip, and I let him pull me between his legs. I chewed on the corner of my lip, waiting. Wanting him to kiss me. Hoping that he was terrible at it so I could purge the ache in my belly.

But I never got the chance.

Without warning, the sky opened up and fell upon us. My ears heard the water droplets bounce against the metal of his truck before my skin registered the cold rain hitting it.

Josh jumped off the tailgate and took my hand, pulling me close behind him. He shoved me into the backseat, slid in beside me, and shut the door.

My skin pricked, goosebumps peppering my flesh. Josh noticed and leaned over the center console to stick the key in the ignition and then turned the heat to full blast. He hit the radio, playing a local country station and a song I had never heard before.

"Better?" Josh asked, falling back into the seat beside me.

"Yeah, thanks."

The back seat of his truck was that of any car, big enough to fit three people, but for some reason, it felt small. Before the first song ended, I was sweating, probably from the hot air but possibly because being beside him made me nervous.

"So, how long are you here for?"

"Um. Just the night, I guess."

Josh frowned and shook his head. "You're going back to Georgia tomorrow? That sucks."

If I could, I'd never go back to Georgia. I loved my family, but with me being a colossal disappointment by not marrying their hand-picked trust fund kid right out of high school, they were too much. I knew I needed to return home for Christmas, but I wasn't going back early unless I absolutely had to.

I smirked, keeping the secret that I had moved to Florida a few months ago to myself. "It does?"

"Yeah. I mean, it seems like every time I finally get to see you, you've got one foot out the door. It would be nice to spend some time with you."

"Really?" I took the hair tie off my wrist and pulled my locks into a ponytail. Having my hair off my neck felt better. Cooler. Lord knew I needed to cool off.

"Well, yeah. Like you said, you're not like the girls around here."

"You don't know what I'm like." I sat back again and looked Josh in the eyes. "You don't know me."

"True." He shifted, angling to face me better. He had this look, one that said he wanted to touch me, but I had taken his chance away by pulling up my hair. "I'd like to, though. What time are you leaving tomorrow?"

I didn't know. I didn't even know for certain where I was staying tonight. I assumed with Hattie since she had driven me here, but we had never talked about it. Now that I thought about things, I was essentially stranded in a strange town with nothing but my phone, ID, and a debit card that barely had enough money on it for a McDonald's meal.

I swallowed hard and pushed all of that aside. Everything would work out. It had to. "After lunch, I think. Hattie drove me, so I'm at her mercy."

Josh grinned, and my heart fluttered faster. His strong jawline made his smile breathtaking. "Hattie will sleep until noon after a night like tonight. Do you want to hang out in the morning before you leave?"

"Sure. What did you have in mind?"

The radio played, warding away any lingering awkwardness as Layla and I rode across town but my stomach was in knots. I didn't get worked up over girls, but I also didn't pick them up for a day date. Not that this could be called a date, but I was hoping to get there.

I tossed and turned all night, unable to sleep. My mind had run through a dozen scenarios for what to do this morning. When I asked Layla to hang out today, I hoped she'd say yes, but I figured she'd shoot me down. Never in a million years did I think I'd get two days with her.

When the light turned red, I lifted the center console, eliminating the barrier between us. Layla looked at me, the corners of her mouth turning up as she slid into the newly created middle seat.

"So," she started, breaking the ice. "You're a bull rider?"

"You remember that?" I fought a smile, both amused and horrified. To say that wasn't my finest moment was an understatement. "I was, but I quit when I accepted a spot on UCF's football team a few years back. All it takes is one bad bull to fuck up your day, but then my brother said he was leaving for medical school and, well, you know the rest."

"I don't understand. What does he have to do with anything?"

"Someone needed to stay behind and help Paw with the ranch. I drew the short straw, so to speak."

Layla chewed on her bottom lip, mulling over my words. I didn't tell her the last bull I rode had bucked me off and almost snapped my neck. I had two hairline fractures on my spine, a major concussion, and a headache that had lasted for weeks. I didn't need the doctors to tell me how lucky I was or how stupid it would be to climb onto that beast again.

"If you're not a bull rider, then why did you use that line on me?"

"Because." I smirked. This chick was under my skin. In one day, she had managed to do what girls had been trying to do for years: spark my interest. She had taken over my mind, weaseled her way into my thoughts, and given me a dose of metaphorical blue balls I wasn't ready for. Sitting next to her, I felt it again—that spark of interest. "If I wanted to ride a bull again, I could. Besides, that line's never let me down before."

"It didn't work on me. I guess it's not a sure thing anymore." She snickered.

I shook my head. The girl had guts. I liked it. "I guess not. What time are you flying back to Georgia tomorrow?"

Layla turned her head toward the window again and bit the corner of her lip. She was fighting a smile and it was hot as hell. "Who said I was going back to Georgia?"

"You did. Last night."

She looked at me, letting that lip slip from between her teeth, unable to fight her grin any longer. "Did I, though?"

"If you're not flying back to Georgia tomorrow, where are you going?"

"To work."

Work?

That told me nothing. I racked my brain trying to pick apart our conversation last night. Hattie had driven Layla, which meant she couldn't live more than a few hours from here. I doubted she was hopping on a plane tonight and going to work tomorrow, which meant she probably lived in Florida. Possibly somewhere nearby.

I rolled the windows down and twisted my fingers in the breeze. I knew better than to get excited. Every time I let myself look forward to something, like the prospect of seeing Layla again, life shit all over my plans. "What do you do?"

"I've been working for my aunt's fundraising company. You'd be surprised how long it takes to set up an event from start to finish." She rolled her window up and ran her fingers through her hair. I tucked my elbow in and rolled mine up, too, because I didn't want to seem like a jerk.

"Oh?" I didn't know shit about fundraisers. My knowledge went about as far as showing up and handing them my money.

"Yeah, the one we've got on Thursday has been a beast. It's taken four months to get everything in order." She turned her head to look out the window, a frown tugging at her lips. "Where are we?"

We were in the middle of nowhere, surrounded by large stretches of open land and pines. My tires crossed off the pavement and onto a poorly graded road. Coins in my cup holders rattled and the glasses hanging from my rearview mirror swung like a pendulum as my tire sank into a hole with a thud and we bounced in our seats. If not for the belts strapping us in, we'd have been slung around like a forgotten bullet in a pair of pants in the dryer.

After about fifteen minutes of bouncing, we reached the gate to Sam's dad's place. He had a nice chunk of land, ten acres, but my ranch was bigger. In fact, my family's property was only thirty more minutes down this road.

So, why wasn't I taking Layla there?

For one, I didn't bring girls home. Unless they were coming to our annual Fourth of July party and had been invited by someone other than me, my bros were the only people to ever walk on my land.

I wasn't embarrassed about where I lived. We had two houses on the property: Paw's, which was close to the barn, and then Mom's house. The land had been in the family for three generations and our family had been here for so long that my great-grandfather's name was on one of the street signs downtown.

But I had seen how Bret's girlfriends' eyes lit up when he brought them around. Some had seen the beauty of our home, while others had seen a fortune and wanted in. We weren't rich by any means, but we weren't poor either. Maintaining the ranch cost a lot of money, more than most people realized, and it was a lot of work, even more so since Paw had passed, but it had been his pride and joy. I'd be damned if it went to some yuppie because Mom couldn't handle it herself and Bret was off chasing tail.

Sam's place, on the other hand, could only be considered a ranch on Halloween when things pretended to be what they weren't. They had a dilapidated double-wide and a handful of skinny cows that weren't worth the cost to feed them. I kept my mouth shut, though, because those cows weren't my problem, and Sam had nothing to do with his dad. The only thing this place had going for it, besides the acreage, was that they had a killer barn.

Crossing over Sam's cattle grate, I veered to the left of the property and parked beside the pole barn. I turned the truck off but left the keys in the ignition. "You ready for this?"

Layla looked around, her eyes slowly taking in the scenery. "What are we doing?"

I bit back a grin, knowing exactly what she saw—a herd of cows, too many acres of grass to mow without a tractor, and a sun-faded trailer. I hoped she didn't think we were white trash. This might not have been my piece of land, but it was my way of life.

I put my arm around Layla's waist and linked her fingers with mine. It was the first move I'd made, and she didn't seem to mind, which gave me hope. "So, around here," I said as we neared the shed behind Sam's trailer, "when there's nothing to do, we blow shit up."

Layla's mouth fell open. I slipped a finger under her chin and pushed it closed. Her eyes met mine for a second and those plump red lips lifted at the corner. I waited, searching for some sign that it was okay to make my next move. I didn't normally think this much. I took what I wanted—a pretty smile usually my invitation—but Layla made me nervous. There was something about her that made me want to try. Something that made me scared to fuck this up.

"Are y'all gonna stare at each other all day? Or are we gonna shoot?"

I tore my gaze away from Layla and found Sam about a foot away, holding my .308 rifle out. Taking a step back from Layla, I grabbed my gun. Sam shook his head, a cocky smirk on his face, then leaned against the side of the shed, his twelve-gauge shotgun beside him.

"We're out of things to safely blow up." I walked to the firing line. Layla followed, stopping beside me as I reached the black spray-painted line that marked a hundred yards from the targets. "So, the next best thing is to shoot something."

I raised my rifle to my shoulder and aimed. I was ready to shoot but held off, glancing over at Layla. She bit her lip, those eyes giving me a once-over she probably thought I couldn't see. "Might want to cover your ears. It's pretty loud."

Layla's delicate hands reached up to cover her ears, and I aimed again.

BANG.

My shoulder hitched from the kick, but after years of hunting, I was used to it. I re-chambered and fired a few more times, hitting each target until the gun clicked, signaling I was out of rounds. Taking a few steps back, I turned and handed Sam the gun.

Layla looked like a puppy that had just found the biggest steak of its life—excited but intimidated. I waved her over and she ran to my side. When we reached the table where Sam set our targets, her gaze flicked across the exploded water bottles. "Dang, not too shabby."

I knew I was a good shot, but it was nice to hear her praise. "Thanks."

We replaced the busted bottles with fresh ones, then walked back to the safety of the shed. Once we were out of the way, Sam raised the shotgun and fired at his targets. Layla watched him, fascination dancing across her face, even though she flinched with each shot.

I wrapped my hand around her waist and pulled her close. She rested her cheek against my shoulder, fingers playing at the hem of my shirt. We stayed like that, watching Sam cross the field and walk to the tables.

I looked down at Layla, but before I could say anything she pressed her mouth against mine, both hands wrapping around my neck. I froze for a second, but then I got my bearings and pulled her closer. Her lips parted, tongue sweeping past mine, and she let out a tiny whimper.

Sam cleared his throat and I swear I could have killed him. Layla's lips left mine, but I didn't let her go. She spun in my arms, resting her head against my chest, and said, "Hey, Sam," like nothing had ever happened.

Josh didn't seem interested in shooting anymore, not since I kissed him. I wasn't sure why I did it. I'd never been forward like that, but when I saw him shoot, that ball of nerves I'd been wrestling with since last night unraveled.

My lips tingled, desperate to know what his felt like, and I gave in. I didn't know what I expected to happen by kissing Josh. I'd kissed Ashley, my ex-boyfriend, dozens of times, with and without tongue, and it had always felt the same. Empty. My mind would wander, counting down the seconds until it was over.

With Josh, I felt everything. Every hair on my body standing on edge. Every butterfly dancing in my stomach. Every electrical surge my brain sent coursing through my body. I felt it all, and it was better than any drug I had tried—which hadn't been a lot—but still. Worse yet, I felt it stop the moment his lips left mine.

Sam held the shotgun out to Josh, silently suggesting it was his turn, but Josh shook his head and nuzzled into my neck, his lips nipping at my ear. "I'm good."

I shuddered, closing my eyes to enjoy the roller coaster inside me. Had I known that kissing Josh would feel this good, I would have done it last March, before I left, and returned his calls. Instead, I dodged the man because he made my heart race in a way that didn't feel natural.

Sam finished resetting the targets for another round and then extended the rifle. This time, Josh took it, pulling his body from mine. As much as I craved to be in his arms again, I was excited to watch Josh shoot.

Only he turned to me, excitement in his eyes, and said, "Your turn."

My jaw went slack. He was joking. There was no way Josh expected me to shoot and hit something on purpose. I shook my head, holding my hands up in protest. "Oh, no. I don't think so."

Josh opened his mouth to argue but changed his mind. Without warning, he crouched and took me by the legs, flipping me over his shoulder. I screamed in playful irritation, not expecting to be lifted off the ground.

My screams quickly turned to laughter as Josh carried me into the field. He set me back on my feet, one hand sliding up my thigh to my lower back, leaving a trail of goosebumps in its wake. Josh remained still, devouring me with his eyes, and I felt it again. That fire growing inside me.

"Any day now!" Sam shouted, breaking the trance we were in.

Josh cleared his throat and took a step back. He walked to a black duffel bag resting on the ground and propped the rifle on top of it. I watched wordlessly as he lay on his belly, then closed one eye to look through a small black cylinder on the top of the gun. Satisfied with what he saw, he turned his attention to me and patted the grass beside him. "Come on."

On the outside, I walked over to him with confidence and grace. On the inside, my stomach churned, my heart raced, and the little voice in my head begged me not to get down on the ground. I didn't listen. I swallowed that knot in my throat and lay on the prickly, half-dead grass.

"This rifle is a .308," Josh said, his eyes flicking to the gun and then back to me. "It doesn't have as much kick as a shotgun, but it can still leave a bruise if you're not careful."

"Great," I mumbled. I'd never shot a Nerf gun, let alone something that used real bullets. This was going to be a disaster.

"I want you to shoot this lying down so the duffel bag takes most of the shock." Josh looked over his shoulder at my backside and grinned. "Also, I don't want you falling on your ass. That bit there..." He pointed to the black cylindrical piece on top of the gun. "You're going to look through it. It's called a scope. You need to line up the 'T' you'll see when you look through it with your target. That's called the crosshairs. Pull the trigger once your target is in the center of the crosshairs."

"Got it."

I sucked in a breath and held it for a few heartbeats, hoping my nerves would settle, then let it out. My body quivered as I closed one eye and looked through the scope. Lining up one of the bottles in the crosshairs, I drew in a quick breath and then pulled the trigger.

The blast was louder up close than I expected. My ears rang and my shoulder throbbed from the kick. I couldn't imagine what it would have felt like standing up. If this one wasn't as bad as the shotgun, I never wanted to shoot that thing.

Josh moved the gun from the duffel bag to the ground beside him. "Well." He rubbed the nape of his neck. "That's one way to do it."

I rolled up onto my knees and brushed the dirt off my thighs. "What do you mean?"

"You'd have a better chance of not missing the target if you keep your eyes open," he said through a chuckle.

I missed? The bottle was lined up. I should have hit it.

Josh stood and then extended a hand to help me to my feet.

My legs were shaky. I wasn't sure if it was from how he made me feel or from lying on the grass. "Want to shoot again?"

I shook my head.

Josh rubbed at the back of his neck, then chuckled again. He took a few steps and then looked over his shoulder. "I'm gonna go check on the targets."

"Uh...okay."

Not sure what to do, but knowing that I didn't belong in the middle of the field, I turned and walked back toward the truck.

"You need to just get it over with," Sam said as I approached. He leaned against the shed, arms lazily crossed in front of him.

"I don't know what you're talking about."

I really didn't have a clue. I had already kissed Josh, so he couldn't be talking about that. And I knew Sam wasn't suggesting we sleep together after one weekend. If he was, these boys had another thing coming. I didn't know what kind of girls they were used to, but I didn't spread my legs easily. It had taken Ashley and me three years to get to that point, and the handful of times we did it were nothing but painful, sometimes bloody, disappointments.

"All right, be that way, but you'll give in to him eventually. I can see it already, even if you can't."

Sam's words made me nervous. Was my attraction to Josh that obvious? "Whatever you think you're seeing, you're wrong. Josh and I are just friends."

Friends that kissed. No big deal. Right?

"Whatever you say, sunshine." Sam pushed off the shed when Josh ambled back toward us. He left me alone to wonder how obvious I was and if I should tone things down.

I didn't have long to think before the bang of one gun and then the other made me lose my train of thought. Both Josh and Sam had guns in hand, and they took turns shooting until they ran out of targets.

The guys laughed, having a moment I wasn't a part of. Back home, with Ashley and his friends, I never felt like I belonged with them, but things were different here. I couldn't explain it, but there was a comforting feeling I'd never felt before. It was even stronger when I was in Josh's arms.

Josh and Sam raced across the grass to the table, nearly barreling into it. They picked up the busted targets, threw them at each other, and then had to pick them up again and tossed them into a bucket. Once everything was cleaned, they strode back toward me, Sam carried the waste, and Josh was laughing at something else I couldn't hear.

"Sam." Josh slapped him on the back when they got close. "It's been real, and it's been fun, but it hasn't been real fun."

Sam snickered and pulled Josh in for a man-hug. "See you later, brother." Sam tipped his hat at me. "Layla, until next time, darlin'."

"So," Josh said, his voice husky and low as he drove me back to Hattie's house. "What are the chances of me seeing you again?"

"I..." My chest constricted, each breath becoming a struggle. Somewhere deep inside, I knew if I gave in to these emotions, Josh was going to change me. I just wasn't sure if it was going to be a good change or not. "I don't know, slim."

Josh's jaw hardened. He paused, gazing off into the distance. We pulled into the grassy knoll beside Hattie's house, and Josh shifted the truck into the park. He sat back in the seat, the engine still running, and stared at the tiny house before us. I waited, unsure if I should stay or go because I wanted to do both.

Josh nodded, thinking to himself, then grabbed his phone off the magnetic holder on the dash. "Can I have your number again?"

"Yeah." I let out a breathy laugh, easing the tension in my chest. With trembling hands, I took the phone from him and typed my number in under the name "the sexiest girl you've ever met." It was a bold move, but when I handed Josh his phone, a smile tugged at his lips.

"Yes, ma'am, you are." He texted me and my phone dinged in my back pocket. His finger brushed against my cheek, touching me delicately, like a rose petal he didn't want to bruise. I looked into his eyes, my breath catching in my throat.

Josh leaned across the armrest and pressed his lips to mine again. There was no tongue with this kiss, but that didn't mean there wasn't a swarm of butterflies going crazy inside me.

All too soon, he pulled back and rested his forehead against mine. I kept my eyes closed, knowing that if I opened them, I'd give into the temptation to kiss him again, really kiss him, and then there was no telling how far I'd go.

Josh backed away and the car door shut before I could lift my eyelids. I looked up and saw him running around the front of the truck. He opened the passenger door for me. I unclicked my seat belt and took the outstretched hand. He closed my door and walked me up Hattie's driveway.

When we reached the front of the house, he tucked his hands in his pockets and said, "I'm glad we got to spend the morning together."

"Me too."

He leaned in, pressing another quick kiss to my lips before saying, "Bye" and walking away.

I t wasn't easy, but I convinced Hattie to tell me what city she picked Layla up from, which was a lifesaver because there are five fundraisers within a hundred miles of Fellsmere tonight.

But only one was in Orlando.

A benefit for a local girl who'd been diagnosed with Cystic Fibrosis. Tickets ranged from seventy-five dollars to two hundred and fifty. Each. I was prepared to spend that and more if I had to to get through the door. A door I quickly discovered was sold out.

But one of their patrons had called in sick, letting the foundation know there would be an open seat if they could sell an additional ticket. That was how I got my foot in the door. Hearing my southern drawl this morning, the woman on the phone made it a point to tell me this was a formal event.

Three times.

So, I pulled my suit from prom out of the closet, squeezed into it as best I could, and drove the hour and a half to surprise a chick who had barely responded to me all week.

Layla had better feel loved.

Every space in the designated parking lot was taken when I got to the venue. I circled the lot and the adjacent street before finding an open spot behind a red Mercedes-Benz on a side alley. I grabbed the bouquet from my passenger seat and followed a stream of people to the event. After checking in at a table near the entrance, I was given a card with my table assign-ment and allowed to enter.

The ballroom they chose tonight was brightly lit with pastel pink accent lights climbing the walls. There were at least a dozen round tables scattered about, covered with white table-cloths, sequin overlays, vases filled with water, and flowers on top of it all. I felt like I was at a wedding, not a benefit. Then again, I'd never been to a fundraiser like this before. Maybe this was how the other half rolled.

Surrounded by people who probably had more money than God, I felt out of place. My suit, with its dark slacks, white button-down shirt, and tie, made me look like I was a part of the crowd. However, like a shark finding blood in the water, somehow these people knew I didn't belong. They stepped to the side as I approached the bar, acting like I had the plague. It was evident that I was out of my league here, but being the underdog has never stopped me from going after what I wanted.

"What can I get you?" the bartender asked, not bothering to look up from the cocktail he was mixing.

"Jack and Coke, please."

The guy handed me my drink, and I walked back toward my table. Pressing the cup to my lips, I swallowed the whiskey in one gulp, welcoming the burn. This was going to be a long night.

"Good evening. If everyone could please find their tables, we'd like to get started," a cheery voice called through the speakers.

Layla stood at a podium on the stage, smiling at the crowd. Her eyes flit across the room, bouncing from one person to another until they stopped on me. Her gaze fell to her papers, cheeks flushing red, before her eyes darted up again.

"Thank you all for coming tonight. As you all know, Mary Herbert was diagnosed with Cystic Fibrosis last summer, a week before her eighth birthday. Cystic Fibrosis is a terrible disease that damages the lungs and digestive system. While scientists have had many breakthroughs, there is still no known cure, and medications are costly. All proceeds from tonight's auction will go towards Mary's never-ending medical bills." Layla paused, letting the crowd whisper amongst themselves before adding, "And now, I'm going to turn the stage over to Hank. Let the auction begin!"

The room erupted in applause as Layla stepped to the side of the stage. The auctioneer, Hank, rambled off words and numbers at an alarming speed while the runner delivered basket after basket to the highest bidders. Two hours later, the auction ended, and everyone was allowed to mingle again.

Layla skirted across the room to shake hands with patrons, eventually making her way over to me. "What are you doing here?" she asks, her arms wrapping around my neck for a brief hug.

"I thought I'd surprise you." I grabbed the bouquet from under my seat and handed it to her. She bit her lip, surprise dancing in her eyes.

"You're sweet." Layla looked behind her as an older woman called her name. The woman frowned and beckoned her with a wave. "I should get back to making my rounds, but I'm glad you came." She turned, heading back to her guests, then looked over her shoulder to add, "Don't leave before saying goodbye. Okay?"

~

"I'm exhausted." Layla saged into the chair next to me. The fundraiser ended over an hour ago, but I stuck around to help with the cleanup. "You didn't have to stay. Don't get me wrong, your man-strength was amazing, but you have over an hour's drive tonight."

I chuckled, never having heard the phrase *man-strength* before.

I liked it.

Hell, Layla could have called me a wuss, and I probably would have liked it because that meant she was thinking about me. Every moment I was on her mind was one more crack in the wall she'd built to keep me out. Sooner or later, I'd break through it. "Each back-breaking minute was worth it since I got to spend more time with you."

Layla threw a dirty napkin at me and grinned. She grabbed her bottle of water and took a sip, then closed her eyes and dropped her head against the back of the chair.

"So, about tomorrow..."

"What about tomorrow?" she asked, eyes still closed.

Reaching both arms above my neck, I stretched, a yawn escaping me. I was beat. One of the heifers gave birth today, but the calf got stuck. I had to physically yank the baby out so both of them wouldn't die. Less than five minutes later, I was panting on the ground, covered in placenta and blood, while both mom and baby trotted off like nothing happened.

That was only a blip of my morning. The rest of the day was everyday ranch work. Come daybreak, I'd be out there again, feeding the horses and tending to the never-ending bullshit. Thankfully, my day worker was on duty this weekend because I needed a break.

"Now that the fundraiser is over and just about everything is picked up, how about coming to spend the weekend with me?"

"Are we back to this?"

"Yup."

Layla opened her eyes and sat upright. She chewed on her bottom lip and stared at me. "You're not going to give up, are you?"

I met her gaze with a grin and shook my head. I'd never

tried this hard to land a chick, but no one had put me under a spell the way Layla had. It wasn't even about sex. Although, I wouldn't complain if she wanted to do that dance. I wanted to spend time with her, get to know her, and see where things would go from there. "Nope."

She stood and dropped the tablecloth into the box by her feet. "I can't afford a hotel room."

"Then stay with me." Like I'd let her stay anywhere else. I pulled the cover off the chair she was in, then stood to grab mine.

"Josh." She frowned, fighting the war written all over her face. She wanted this. I knew she did, but something was holding her back. "Do you really think that's a good idea?"

"Don't lift those. I'll get them." I shooed her away from the stack of chairs she tried to lift and then carried them across the room. When I was done, I met her at the following table, and we started the cleanup process again. "You can take my room and I'll sleep on the couch. I'll probably be up before you anyway to feed the horses. With me in the living room, I won't disturb you."

"Fine, but not tonight. I've got a few things to finish up in the morning." Layla wiped the sweat from her brow and leaned against the table. "I can meet you around four."

"Four is good. I'll text you my address in the morning."

"Perfect." Layla reached out and touched my arm. "You should get going, Josh. You have a long drive ahead of you."

I stepped in front of Layla, one leg on either side of her. She looked at me and sucked in an audible breath. I threaded my fingers through the hair at the base of her neck and pressed my mouth to hers for a quick kiss. I'd love to deepen it and fully taste those lips, but I wanted her to think about me tonight.

"Goodnight, beautiful. See you tomorrow."

My stomach felt like it was on a roller coaster, lifting high into my throat as I got closer to Josh's place, then dropping down into my seat as I passed it. I'd driven down his dirt road, passed the turnoff, then circled back twice, trying to decide if sleeping at his house was a good idea.

I was equally excited and terrified about tonight. I knew Josh had mentioned me staying for the weekend, but I doubted that would happen. One night was more than enough to get a feel for what I was doing because, honestly, I had no clue.

During the week, I spent my days occupying my mind with my classes and fundraising stuff, and even then, he still sneaked into my thoughts. Nights were the worst. I had overanalyzed everything Josh said and did last weekend. I found his Facebook, Instagram, and TikTok accounts, straddling the line between curious and stalker more than once.

All so I could convince myself that these feelings for Josh were a bad idea. I didn't need any distractions and he was proving to be a major one.

So, why couldn't I stop thinking about him?

After two more drive-bys, I finally turned down the bumpy driveway. I passed the first house on the property and followed a narrow, tire-track path through the grass.

Against my better judgment, I stayed on the path, turning around a large barn, and was met with a cute, log cabin-style house. When Josh said he'd sleep on the couch, I had assumed he lived in a tiny cottage like Hattie. This place might not have been some luxurious eight-bedroom home like Aunt Tricia's house, but it wasn't small, either.

I parked my Jetta beside Josh's truck, feeling slightly better now that I recognized his vehicle but unable to force myself to move.

I was out of my comfort zone.

The only guy I had ever been with was Ashley, and I wouldn't have called what we had a healthy relationship.

We didn't date unless I counted social gatherings at the country club with our parents as dates. We didn't go out without my brother as a chaperone. We didn't do anything normal teenagers did because we didn't like each other for ninety percent of our relationship. We had essentially been arranged to be married and forced to get along.

Not once had I felt these nervous flutters that were wreaking havoc inside me when we were together. I had never lost sleep wondering what Ashley was doing or who he was with. And I definitely hadn't had an erotic dream about him that felt so real I had questioned myself the next morning as to whether it had actually happened.

All of this couldn't be normal.

Maybe I was getting sick and should go home.

Maybe...

Knock. Knock. Knock.

I jumped in my seat and looked up. Josh was at my window, lips curling into a smile that reached his eyes. I clicked the unlock button, and he swung my door open.

"Are you going to come inside or sit out here all night?" He extended his hand to help me out of my car and pulled me into a bear hug as soon as I was on my feet.

Josh took a step back after a heartbeat of holding me close, dropped his arms, and smiled. There was a burning sensation of anticipation in my chest, and I found myself blushing again. I pressed the button on my key fob to open my trunk and grabbed my overflowing backpack, but Josh immediately took it from me, swinging it over his shoulder as if it were an empty pillowcase.

He cleared his throat and glanced over at his house. "Come on."

"This is beautiful," I told him, looking around the living room.

The walls were wood-paneled, like the outside, with large windows letting in the Florida sun. The floors were white-tiled, which made the room even brighter. The house felt warm and cozy, and all I wanted to do was curl up on the sofa with a cup of coffee and a book.

"Thanks. It was my paw's place before he passed." Josh kicked his boots off by the door. I reached down and unclasped the strap of my sandals, following his lead, and set my shoes beside his.

"I'll show you to your room."

I followed but stopped to look at a picture in the hallway. Josh doubled back to stand beside me with a mile-wide grin. "That was a good day. That's Paw, and that's Bret, my brother." He then pointed to the picture of a kid missing his two front teeth, holding a fish bigger than his arm. "The stud with the fish is me. I fought that beast for ten minutes before finally reeling it in." He chuckled at the memory. "No sooner did the flash of Paw's camera go off did the fish wiggled out of my hands and flop off the side of the boat."

Josh laughed again, then opened the second door on the left. The room was white-walled instead of wood, but the bed frame and dresser were dark oak, tying it to the rest of the house. To my surprise, his room was spotless, like the house— no dirty clothes on the floor or cups on the nightstand. There wasn't even a speck of dust on the ceiling fan.

"The house has three bedrooms." Josh set my bag on the bed and then leaned against the footboard. "My room, an office, and Paw's room. I don't go into his room, though; it's too hard."

I sat beside Josh and took his hand in mine. I might not have known him well, but I knew what suffering looked like, and he looked like he was hurting. "Were you close?"

"Yeah. My dad wasn't around. He bailed sometime after I was born. Paw took us in. Built this house for Mom, then moved us to the main house when Bret started middle school." Josh fell back onto the bed and stared at the ceiling. "I miss him."

"I'm sorry." I knew apologizing for someone's death never helped, but I didn't know what else to say. I felt bad for having opened a wound that didn't seem old.

"It's life," Josh said with a sigh. "You live, and then you die." He pushed himself off the bed. I stood as he stepped toward the door, unsure if I should give him space or follow.

"I hope you brought something nice to wear."

"I did." Mamma had taught me always to be prepared. While Josh and his friends seemed like the jeans-and-T-shirt kind of people, I grabbed a dress and some heels. Just in case.

"Good, we're going to dinner. Then, if you'd like, I thought we'd hit up Cowboy's."

"What's that?"

"A bar on the outskirts of town. There's usually a band on Friday nights. I thought it could be fun."

Josh reached out and took my hand. He pulled me against his chest, his other arm wrapping around my waist.

I looked up into his eyes, feeling my pulse everywhere. This was what I had been worried about—what would happen if we were alone together in a house and a bedroom. I didn't think I'd sleep with him, but the way my head was swimming, I couldn't say for sure, especially if I had a few drinks tonight.

"That sounds like fun."

"I'm glad you're here." Josh threaded his fingers through my hair, careful not to pull my roots. He dipped his head, lips pressing against mine until I was breathless with a flurry of butterflies in my chest. He gripped my hip, fingers digging into my skin. It hurt, but it was a good kind of hurt that made me want more.

Josh backed us against the wall. His hands fell to my thighs, and he lifted me. He nipped at my shoulder, trailing kisses up my neck until he sucked my earlobe into his mouth.

"Josh," I whispered, never having felt anything like this before.

Josh's tongue brushed across my bottom lip before sweeping into my mouth again. I gripped him tighter with my legs, feeling myself coming undone. My hips rocked instinctively and Josh grunted.

He pulled his lips away and leaned his forehead against mine. "You are going to be my undoing, beautiful."

I untangled my legs from around his body, not sure how to process that, and said, "I should probably get ready," before running away to hide in the bathroom.

Waiting on the couch while Layla got dressed was a strange type of torture. Knowing she was in my room and I couldn't touch her drove me crazy. Trying to distract myself with the nonsense on TV was pointless because Layla was all I could think about.

When she stepped into the living room and my breath caught at the sight of her. She wore a black dress that hugged her chest down to her waist before spilling out over her hips and falling near her knees. She did a little spin, and the hem of her skirt crawled dangerously high on her sun-kissed thighs.

She was absolutely stunning. I watched her for a solid five seconds before I couldn't take it any longer. I took Layla's forearm and pulled her onto the couch. I set my hands on her waist as she settled onto my lap. She bit her lip, and it took all the restraint I had not to suck it into my mouth again.

I leaned forward, my lips brushing against her ear. "You look stunning."

Layla giggled, pinching her shoulder and cheek together. "Thanks."

I kissed her cheek once but stopped there. We had reservations at six thirty. Things had gotten hot and heavy faster than I expected in the bedroom earlier. I couldn't guarantee that we'd stop in time if we started again. "We should probably get going. It's about a forty-five-minute drive to the restaurant."

LAYLA'S HEELS clicked against the linoleum floor of Thai Heaven, the mom-and-pop restaurant I found during my senior year of high school. The food was cheap but amazing. For fifteen dollars, you got more on your plate than you would at a chain restaurant, paying more than double.

Trong was usually the waitress on duty. She worked in front while her husband, Kim, cooked, but there was a new girl working on the floor I hadn't seen before. The girl was pretty but didn't hold a candle to Layla.

Layla chewed on her bottom lip as she scanned the menu. I stared at her, feeling a nervousness I didn't think I'd ever get used to. "What do you want?"

"I have no clue." She turned the page and found the curry options. "What do you suggest?"

"I like the yellow curry." I reached over and pointed to where it was on the menu. "It's got a little kick, but it isn't bad. Do you like spicy food?"

She shook her head. I flipped her back a page and pointed to my other favorite dish. "You might like this one. The sweet and sour sauce is out of this world. I usually get the tofu to go with it, but they have pork and chicken, too."

Our waitress came back to the table with her order pad in hand. She batted her eyelashes, an inviting smile on her face that I was doing my best to ignore. I wasn't interested and the last thing I wanted was to give her mixed signals. "Do you know what you want?"

"I think I need a few more minutes." Layla raised her gaze to meet our waitress' but the girl had set her sights on me.

She pushed her chest closer to my face and slipped a piece of paper, presumably with her number on it, into my shirt pocket. "Whatever you need, baby, I'm more than happy to give it to you."

"Mmm-hmmm." I stared at my menu like it was made of gold. The woman had guts; I'd give her that, but no tact. As soon as she walked away, I took the paper out of my pocket, crumpled it into a ball, and dropped it on the floor.

Layla eyed me curiously, the gears visibly turning inside her beautiful mind. "Did she give you her number?"

"Don't know." I shrugged and closed my menu. "I didn't look."

Layla's jaw fell open like she was going to say something, but she changed her mind and snapped her mouth shut. She took another minute to read over the dinner options, then closed her menu.

"You know what you want?" I asked.

"Yeah, I think I'll try the tofu you suggested." She sighed, then frowned. "I wish I had a sweet tea."

It dawned on me that our waitress had me brought my usual lemonade but hadn't asked Layla what she wanted to drink or even gotten her water.

"I'll be right back." I grabbed her menu and mine then walked to the back of the restaurant and toward the kitchen. I pushed the swinging door open, and as expected, Kim was at the stove.

"Josh," he said with a grin, tossing some vegetables in his wok. "How are you doing?"

"I'm good, man. Real good." I 'd come here once a week for the past four years, building a relationship with Trong and Kim. Back then, they were a new restaurant and had time to chat. Now, they were slammed six days a week. The man was hustling and killing it, so I didn't want to take up too much of his time. "Listen, man, your new waitress gave me her number in front of my date."

"A date?" Kim grinned and pushed the swinging door open to peer into the dining room. "The girl in the black?"

"Yeah." I rubbed the back of my neck. Only one girl was

sitting by herself at a two-person table. It wasn't hard to figure out who I was here with, but that didn't make me any less anxious. "That's her."

"She's hot." Kim walked back to the stove and started serving someone's order. "I'll have a word with Tamra. Do you know what you want to eat?"

"Yeah. I'll have my usual, the yellow curry, and she'd like the tofu sweet and sour." I grabbed a pen from the table by the door and wrote our order on a scrap of paper. "Thanks, Kim."

"Anything for our best customer." Kim set the finished plates on a tray and then began working on his next order.

"Hey, do you mind if I grab my girl a sweet tea?"

"Sure. Go for it."

I left the kitchen and walked behind the bar. My waitress, who I assumed was Tamra, cornered me as I was filling Layla's cup. "What are you doing?"

"Kim wants to talk to you," I said, then walked around the counter without glancing at her and grabbed the pitcher of tea.

"You can't do that!" Tamra yelled as I filled a cup, but I ignored her.

Back at the table, I set Layla's tea in front of her. She looked up at me, wide-eyed, with a grin. "Where'd you go?"

I pulled my chair out and sat again. "I'm friends with the owner. We won't have any more problems tonight."

Layla smiled again and took a sip of her tea. It must not have been sweet enough because she opened a packet of sugar and dumped it in. Or maybe I had grabbed unsweet by mistake.

Tamra dropped our plates on the table a few minutes later and walked away without saying a word. Layla picked up her fork and dove in. She looked up every now and then and smiled, but I couldn't help feeling the tension build between us.

"I'm not very good at this," I admitted, rubbing the back of my neck. "Honestly, I haven't taken a girl on a proper date in years."

Layla's green eyes widened. She swallowed the bite in her mouth and asked, "Really?"

"There hasn't been anyone I've wanted to get to know outside of the bedroom since high school." I grimaced, realizing that sounded better in my head than it did out loud.

"But you've had girlfriends before, right?" She leaned back in her chair, a tiny crease forming between her brows.

"Define 'girlfriend'."

Layla looked at me, horrified, and I chuckled. "Don't judge me. Those girls knew from day one that I didn't want anything serious. If they got hurt, then that's on them."

Her eyes narrowed. "And what do you want from me?"

That was the question of the day. What did I want from Layla?

I knew what I didn't want: I didn't want Layla with anybody else, and that was a first. Normally, I didn't care about what a girl did or who they did it with, but the thought of any man's hands on her made me see red. "Truthfully, I don't know."

"Huh," she said, taking a bite of rice and vegetables.

I dropped my gaze, waiting for her to say something other than "huh." Seconds turned into minutes, the silence eating away at me. I was dying to know...

What did she want out of this?

The front parking lot of Cowboy's was packed. Josh drove around the back of the building and made his own parking space in a vacant lot beside a few other trucks. Never in my life had I been with someone who made their own parking space. Ashley had always valeted his cars, and so had my mother.

Getting out, I wobbled. My heels sank into the grass with each step. Josh must have seen me struggling because he put a supportive arm around my waist, ushering me out of the grassy lot and onto the sidewalk. Nestled close to his body, the scent of his cologne was heavenly. It was the kind of smell that made me want to bury my nose in his chest and not come up for air. I didn't, but I wanted to.

"Sorry." Josh shot me an apologetic look as we approached the front of the building. Landon, Hattie, and Sam were huddled in a group, likely waiting for our arrival. "Sam must have opened his mouth about us coming here tonight."

"It's fine." I enjoyed our alone time, but being around his friends was fun, too. They were nothing like my friends back home. We'd get together after school to study sometimes, but we never hung out. Josh's hand slid from around my waist down my arm until our fingers tangled together.

"What's up, man?" Landon, Hattie's boyfriend, held his hand up.

"Not much." Josh high-fived Landon, then slapped Sam

across the stomach, who then punched him in the shoulder. I rolled my eyes. Boys.

A big man in a black shirt that said "Bouncer" blocked the front entrance, carding people before allowing them inside. I dug through my purse and realized I had left my fake ID some-where. Hopefully, it was in my apartment and not in my jewelry box in Georgia. Out of time and options, I held out my real ID and extended my hand. The bouncer put a big black X on it with a permanent marker.

Josh chuckled. He leaned in, his breath tickling my ear, and said, "Don't worry, beautiful. I'm not drinking tonight. I'll get you whatever you want."

Cowboy's was nothing like the nightclubs I had been to in Atlanta. Those were tiered, with bars lining the walls, while the rest of the room was an open space. Music was funneled through speakers, and each floor had its own theme. Even though I had only been twice and was chaperoned by my brother, I had a great time.

This building was one large space divided into three sections. To my left was an L-shaped bar with a dozen or so high-top chairs. On my right was a game area with four red pool tables, three dartboards, and a sign pointing toward the bathrooms. Then, straight ahead, was a stage and a dance floor full of people in boots and jeans. A nervous noose wrapped itself around my stomach. Not only was I the only one of us with the black X of doom on my hand, but I was also over-dressed.

As if Josh could read my thoughts, he leaned in to yell over the music, "You are the most beautiful girl here." He kissed my cheek with a whisper of a touch before pulling away. "Go with the guys. I'll catch up in a minute."

Hattie took Josh's place beside me as soon as he stepped out of reach and took my hand. "Come dance with me!"

"Oh, no." I shook my head. "I'm liable to sprain my ankle in these shoes. You go. Have fun."

Hattie jutted her bottom lip, faking disappointment, then turned on her heels. She skipped to the dance floor and jumped into a line dance routine. I watched her for a second, trying to pick up the steps, but there were too many kicks and turns. I had been a gymnast for most of my childhood. I knew how to count rhythm and could easily fall into a routine, but watching Hattie out there made my head spin.

I climbed the three steps to where the pool tables were and found Sam and Landon engaged in a heated game of rock, paper, scissors by the dartboard. Landon won, crushing Sam's scissors with his rock, so he threw first. He missed by a mile, sticking the dart into the drywall beside the board.

Josh appeared a few minutes later, a large red drink with a miniature umbrella in one hand and what looked like a soda in his other. He handed me the red one. "I think you'll like this."

I looked up at him, straw between my lips, and took a sip. He was right—it was delicious—but my mind was miles away from my drink. It was tumbling down the rabbit hole, wondering how he knew about whatever this drink was called, who he had bought it for before, and why he was here with me.

Deep down, I knew this would never work, not in the long term, but I couldn't bring myself to walk away.

My pulse drummed in my ears, and I wondered if he would kiss me again. Better yet, did I want him to kiss me again?

That was a stupid question. Josh was the best kisser I had ever had. Granted, I had only kissed three people, but he was at the top of the list. I could only imagine what he'd be like in bed. My cheeks heated at that thought. I bet he was great.

The slurping of my straw startled me. I looked down at my

empty cup, wondering where it had all gone and why I was thinking about sleeping with Josh.

"Josh!" Landon hollered across the pool table. He grabbed two cues and held one out for him to take. "Get in on this game."

"Nah, man. I'm good." Josh shook his head and looked at my glass. He smirked and then took it from my hand. "I'm gonna grab her another drink."

"Don't be such a little bitch," Landon countered. "She won't mind. You don't mind, right, Layla?"

Did I want my date to leave me to play a game that took his attention off me? No, but these were his friends. I didn't want any resentment from them or, worse, to have Josh feel like he had to hang out with me. "Of course not."

"I'll be right back," Josh yelled over his shoulder as he walked down the steps to the bar.

I glanced across the room and found Hattie still doing her thing on the dance floor. I could watch her move for hours, laughing like she didn't have a care in the world, even when she messed up.

I jumped in my seat when someone touched my leg. Josh was back, quicker than I expected, with another red drink. I placed the straw between my lips, and he smirked as soon as he handed it over.

"Dude." Landon threw his hands up and then pointed to the pool table.

I wrinkled my brows when I heard the slurping of my straw again. There had to be a hole at the bottom of this cup because there was no way I had sucked it down so fast. "Go on. I need to go to the bathroom anyway."

"I'll be here when you get back." Josh dipped his head and kissed my lips. I didn't get time to relish them because he pulled away a fraction of a second later and turned toward Landon. "You're going down, Landon."

I waited in line, bouncing on my toes to not think about the urgent need to pee, for about ten minutes before a stall opened. You'd think that a place as busy as this would have more than three toilets in the girl's bathroom, but no.

As luck would have it, it was the handicapped one that was free. I looked behind me to see if anyone needed the oversized stall more than I did. No one made a move for the big stall, so I went in.

I did my business and looked down at the X as I washed my hands. The soap had already faded the black marker. If I scrubbed a little harder, the ink would barely be visible. I pumped more soap onto the back of my hand and worked my fingernails in a circle over the foam. It took a minute, but the X disappeared. I smiled into the mirror and fixed my hair, proud that I was no longer putting Josh in danger for contributing to a minor.

When I left the restroom, Josh wasn't at the pool table with Landon. I glanced around the game area but couldn't find him.

Nervous needles crept down my spine, but I pushed them away. The last time my *date* disappeared, I caught him with his pants down.

Literally.

I wasn't heartbroken. I didn't love Ashley, but seeing the man who promised himself to me balls deep in another woman hurt. "Did you see where Josh went?"

Hattie, sweaty and out of breath from the dance floor, rubbed an ice cube over the back of her neck and shook her head. "I thought he was with you."

"I was in the bathroom." I bit my lip and looked around again but didn't see him. *Everything is fine. Josh isn't Ashley. Give him the benefit of the doubt.*

"Relax." Hattie rested her hand on my arm. "That man is crazy about you. I doubt he went far."

"I'm gonna go find him."

Hattie gave me a wave, then went back to cooling herself off. I circled the game area, making sure I didn't miss him. Convinced he wasn't there, I stepped down to the main level. I walked around the dance floor and headed toward the bar. Just when I thought all hope was lost, I caught a glimpse of Josh, heading into a room marked employees only, with a gorgeous blonde.

"If you don't come in there with me, I'm going to tell my manager you're buying drinks for a minor," Amanda Harbrough demanded.

I gritted my teeth and followed her through a side door marked *Employees Only* because getting arrested would have looked worse on a first date than disappearing for a few minutes. Although, if either of the guys had seen me duck into a breakroom with Amanda, any and all chances I had with Layla would have been shot. Hattie had taken a liking to her, which meant they'd bust my balls if Layla got hurt.

I crossed my arms as the door closed and glared. Amanda needed to realize that this was the last place on earth I wanted to be. If I had known she'd gotten a job at Cowboy's, Layla and I would never have come here. "What do you want?"

Amanda smiled, gloating because I'd done what she wanted for the first time in weeks. She was pretty with her bleached hair and dark eyeliner, and she knew it. Her confidence was what caught my attention a few months ago when she came on to me. Too bad she was crazier than a sprayed roach. "You haven't been returning my calls."

"And?" I would have blocked her number if I could have figured out how.

I wasn't technologically illiterate, like Mom, but every time

Apple released a new phone, Bret took mine and upgraded both his and mine, not caring if I wanted something new. I was handed something I didn't know how to use, but it made him happy, so I didn't complain. I wasn't a lost cause; I could text, read emails, and work the four apps I used daily, but that was about as far as my smartphone knowledge went.

"And…" Amanda set her hands over her flat stomach. "We have things we need to discuss."

"We." I pointed my finger between us. "Don't need to talk about anything. You…" I pointed at her. "Need to leave me alone."

I turned and grabbed the handle of the breakroom door. I'd entertained her bullshit long enough. That thing growing in her stomach wasn't mine. We'd slept together twice, with condoms, and she was supposed to be on the pill. I was more likely to win the lottery than to spawn a child with those odds. Besides, Amanda was about as well known around town as Kelly, and it wasn't for her good looks.

"This baby is coming whether you like it or not, Josh!" she yelled. "You can live in denial for seven more months, but I know what the paternity test is going to say, so get ready."

I shook my head, more irritated than pissed. This was the reason I never brought girls home. Amanda might not have known what the ranch looked like, but she knew it existed, and she knew it was mine. I'd bet that baby belonged to some crackhead and she was on her knees every night, praying it was mine because I had a stable income.

"Until I see my name on a legal paternity test—not one of those drug store ones—leave me alone. We're done." I stepped into the bar and slammed the door behind me, not that anyone could hear my tantrum over the music.

I stopped at the bar before heading back up to the pool tables. I needed a drink and possibly a restraining order. The bartender handed me a Jack and soda, and I turned, leaning my elbows on the counter. I took a sip and almost spit it all over the guy walking past me.

I hadn't been gone long, ten minutes tops—nowhere near enough time for Layla to slip into someone else's arms on the dance floor. It wasn't just the guy's hand on her back that had me seeing red, nor the fingers he'd threaded through her hair. It was his lips, pressed against hers that made me forget we were at a bar and not a mudhole back home.

I pushed through the room, shoving people out of my way. I wasn't nice about it, earning a few scowls and snide remarks. Someone reached for my shoulder, but I brushed them off because all I could see was the back of Layla's head—thankfully no longer kissing the person in front of her—and the top of the dude's blonde locks.

I reached them and took Layla by the arm, pulling her out of the way because this guy was about to die. I balled my fist but hesitated when I recognized the crooked nose and shit-eating grin. "You son of a bitch."

Sam stumbled back a step, chuckling when I shoved him. "Took you long enough."

"What the hell?" I yelled—at neither of them and both of them at the same time.

I thought Layla was different. She ignored me, shot me down, and gave me hope that not every girl out there was spreading her legs as soon as a good-looking dick came around. I ran my hands through my hair, trying to figure out why I was so pissed and what to do next. "Why were you kissing him?"

Layla gasped, and my tunnel vision widened enough for me to see her tear-stained cheeks and bloodshot eyes. They were too red and puffy for her to have just started crying.

Layla ran past me, her shoulder brushing against my arm as she disappeared to God-knows-where. Sam stepped closer, blocking me from chasing after her, and pointed behind him.

"That chick drove almost two hours to be with you tonight.

She likes you, even if she won't come out and say it yet. And what do you do?" He paused, likely waiting for me to respond. When I didn't, he added, "You decided to ignore her the moment Amanda showed up."

"I don't care about Amanda."

"Yeah?" Sam chortled. "Well, you could have fooled me. Layla saw you sneak into a back room with her. I did, too."

I felt my frustrations boiling inside me. Tonight had gone to shit. Between the drama with Amanda and now this, I was ready to throw in the towel and go home. If Sam wanted to be with Layla so badly, she could stay at his house. I might have liked the girl, but I didn't play with cheaters.

"Amanda was starting drama, as usual, but Layla came here with me and then kissed you. She was the unfaithful one, not me."

I turned to leave, but Sam grabbed my arm. "I convinced Layla to dance with me because she downed two shots of tequila faster than Landon finishes, and we both know his longest lay is thirty seconds. She was spiraling, and that bartender was more than happy to enable her. I kissed her and she pulled back—more upset than before—because she was worried someone would tell you. Even though she was hurting, she didn't want to upset you. Then your shitty ass came down here and started acting like a jealous prick." Sam poked me in the chest with his finger. "Tighten up before I steal your girl for real."

My stomach dropped, the rage I'd felt only a moment ago replaced with shame. "Hell." I ran my hand through my hair and tugged at the roots. I needed to feel something to make sure this wasn't some jacked-up nightmare. It wasn't, and the realization that anything I could have had with Layla was tumbling down the drain gutted me. "I'm messing this up, aren't I?"

"Majorly." Sam rested his hand on my shoulder and looked

me in the eye. "But I think you've still got a chance if you let Hattie run damage control."

"That's probably a good idea." I sighed, pulled Sam in for a hug, and clapped him on the shoulder. I had to tell Layla something if I wanted to save whatever we had going, and Hattie would want answers, too. "Thanks, man. Even though you're a jerk for kissing my girl, I appreciate you looking out."

"Anytime." Sam slapped me on the butt and turned toward the bar. "Now, go get her!"

Sitting on the sticky floor of the handicapped stall in the girls' bathroom wasn't where I thought I'd end up tonight. Yet, there I was, crying my eyes out, ruining the makeup I had worked so hard to make perfect.

"Layla? Are you in here?" a voice echoed. "It's Hattie."

I sucked in a breath, desperate to choke back my tears and be as quiet as possible. I didn't want to talk. I wanted to curl into a ball and disappear.

My first real date had been a disaster. I hadn't thought anything could be worse than going into anaphylactic shock in the middle of my parents' country club the day they announced Ashley and I were in love, but this took the cake.

With Ashley, I worried about embarrassing my family and ruining the partnership they'd worked years to forge through us. Tonight, I felt naïve and betrayed by both Josh and Sam.

"I know you're in here. I can hear your sniffling." Hattie pushed on the stall doors until she reached the one I was in. The lock clanged and reared against itself. She bent down, sticking her head under the door, and frowned. "Open up, or I'm crawling under."

I shifted to stare at the cheap tile on the wall. I wasn't moving until this bar closed and everyone left. I had exactly eighty-seven dollars in my bank account. That should have been enough to get an Uber to Josh's place, where I could grab my car and drive home. There was nothing in that house I couldn't live without. I would rather replace everything in my backpack than see him again.

With a huff, Hattie crawled under the door and found herself a place on the ground beside me. "Ugh, I need a shower now. This floor is nasty." She wrinkled her nose and wiped her hands on her pants as if that would magically make the germs disappear.

A laugh escaped me, but it was choked by a sob. Hattie put an arm around me, and I let my head fall against her shoulder. She didn't try to talk. Instead, she sat there, letting me cry until I ran out of tears.

"He likes you a lot, you know." She ran her fingers through the curls I struggled to make only a few hours ago. They tangled in the hairspray, pulling every now and then, but the pain reminded me that there was more to me than an aching heart. So, I didn't mind.

"Who?"

"Josh."

I shook my head, convinced anything that could have been between Josh and me was ruined. I bit my lip to ease the pain in my chest. I didn't know why this hurt so much. We had shared a handful of kisses, that was all. "He probably thinks I'm a slut for kissing Sam."

Hattie gripped my shoulders and pushed me upright, forcing me to look at her. "First off, Sam is a dog. Everyone knows he can't keep his hands to himself. And Josh wasn't mad at you, just shocked. Although, I'll admit, he should have handled himself better."

"I don't know." I buried my face in my arms and ugly cried again. If knowing the mess I was in was Sam's fault was supposed to make me feel better, it didn't. I was just one of the many girls he had kissed and passed on to his friends. Oh, god. I was sloppy seconds!

"I've been around a while now," Hattie said, rubbing my back, "and I've never seen Josh try this hard. He made me watch him try on eight different outfits today. Eight! All because he wanted to impress you."

I sniffled and looked up at her, the vice grip on my chest loosening. I wanted him to like me, but I needed him to tell me why he had run off with that chick. I refused to be with someone who cheated.

"Josh has a lot on his plate." Hattie wiped the tears from my cheeks with the back of her finger. "Believe me when I say I know he can be hot-headed. He has a temper like no other, but Josh is the most amazing guy I've ever met. If I wasn't with Landon, he's one of the few men I'd consider being with in this county. Give him another chance."

"What about that girl he disappeared with?"

Hattie pulled a handful of toilet paper from the dispenser beside her and handed it to me so I could blow my nose. "She's nothing but a snake. Trust me when I say you have nothing to worry about."

"Layla?" Josh's voice echoed in the bathroom. I froze and stared at Hattie wide-eyed. This was the girls' bathroom, a sacred place, and he invaded it.

I wasn't ready to face him yet.

"We're in here," Hattie called out. She pulled me to my feet and rubbed her thumbs under my eyes. I probably looked like I had gotten into a fight with a raccoon, but not much could be done. "I'll stand guard," she said, opening the stall door for him.

Josh hovered in the entryway of the stall with his hands in his pockets. "I'm sorry. I didn't mean to yell at you."

I leaned against the sink and crossed my arms. I wanted to be mad or even feel the hurt I was drowning in only moments ago, but Josh looked like he had been run over by a truck. I fought the urge to pull him into a hug because all I wanted to do was make him feel better. It was the mother hen complex in me. I had a soft spot for them all: stray dogs, lost cats, and lizards without tails. "Tell me about the girl."

"She's pregnant." Josh ran his fingers through his hair.

I sucked in a breath and it caught. I couldn't let it go. Couldn't feel anything over my heart beating against my chest. "She's what?"

"It's not mine!" Josh insisted, closing the space between us and reaching for me. I let him take my hands because he looked like he might break if I didn't. "We slept together twice, and I used a condom both times. Plus, she was on the pill."

I pulled my hands back and wrapped them around myself. I felt dirty, even though I hadn't done anything wrong. I wasn't a fool. I knew Josh had been with other people, but that didn't mean I wanted to hear about it. I must have made a face because Josh ran his hands through his hair. He backed against the stall and slid down to the floor.

This must have been what Hattie was talking about—the things he had going on. I chewed my bottom lip and watched Josh drop his head onto his arms. I couldn't imagine what he was going through, having someone claim a baby was his. A baby that he was ninety-nine percent sure wasn't, but then there was that one percent haunting him.

I sat down beside him and leaned my shoulder against his.

"I wanted to make a good impression tonight." Josh lifted his head and dropped it against the wall behind him.

"You were batting a thousand at dinner."

"And now?" Josh's sad eyes looked at me.

I didn't know. The whole maybe-baby situation complicated everything. Logically, I knew I should jump ship and get as far away from Josh and his drama as possible, but my heart and my head were out of sync. A part of me wanted to see where this went, and I was having a hard time ignoring it.

The bathroom door swung open, and Hattie hollered, "I hate to interrupt, but we are getting a line out here."

Josh sighed and pulled himself to his feet. He held out a hand for me and said, "Let's go home."

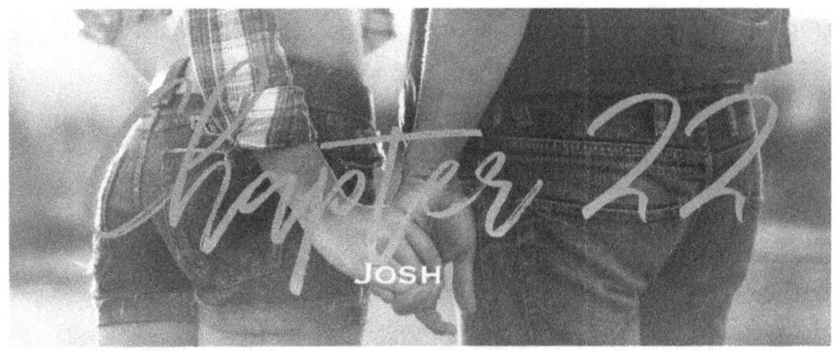

Chapter 22

It had been a long night and sleep seemed unreachable. I was antsy. My mind kept straying, assaulting me with the same question over and over: *How could I have let tonight go so wrong?*

Layla laid on the couch with her head in my lap. Things between us hadn't been the same since Cowboy's. Tension lingered and I didn't know how to ease it.

I ran my fingers through Layla's hair while she picked a movie on Netflix. The strands were soft and smelled like summer and strawberries. Every cell in my body wanted to react to her closeness. Restraining human nature, keeping myself from becoming even the slightest bit hard, was practically impossible. But I was trying.

"So," Layla said, turning in my lap to look at me. "I found my favorite movie, but you'll probably hate it."

Mamma Mia waited on the screen. I recognized it as one Hattie made me watch a few months ago and stifled a groan. I hated musicals, but I'd have given anything to see Layla smile again. So I nodded.

The corners of her lips lifted and she turned back on her side. Her hand shifted under her head and I bit my lip, then exhaled a heavy breath. *I can do this.*

About twenty minutes into the movie, Layla's breathing slowed and her eyes closed. I watched her sleep until the credits rolled, trying to figure out how I could fix things between us. I liked this girl more than I should and I didn't want to screw this up any more than I had. "Layla?"

"Mmm?" she mumbled, eyes still closed.

"Are you sleeping?"

"Mmm," she mumbled again.

I smirked, feeling safe to say what was on my mind. "I won't tell you when you're awake, but I can't stop thinking about you. I've never met anyone who makes me feel things like you do. I get these stupid flutters, and sometimes it's like I can't breathe when you're around. I don't know what you've done to me."

She didn't respond and when Netflix returned to the menu screen, I had to accept the inevitable—it was time to put her in bed. Layla's head fell upon my shoulder as I carried her down the hall to my room. She was light, but that didn't stop me from worrying. Given my bad luck streak tonight, I was liable to trip over my feet and drop her. Thankfully, I didn't, so I used the hand under her legs to pull the comforter back and then lay her down.

Strands of hair splayed across Layla's face when her head found the pillow. I tucked them behind her ear, my fingers trailing across the soft skin of her cheek. She was beautiful. It killed me that I hadn't made her mine yet.

As I closed the door behind me, she asked, "Where are you going?"

I stepped back into the room and leaned against the dresser. "I tried not to wake you."

Layla sat upright, her eyes half open, and bunched her brows together. I smirked because the just-woke-up look wasn't something I'd ever seen on girls, but I would have killed to see it on her again.

"I'm heading to the couch," I clarified.

"Are you sure?" Layla scooted to the side, her gaze darting to the mattress, then back to me. "Pretty sure you could fit an army on this mattress."

I chuckled and strolled across the room. Tiny tremors attacked my muscles. I was shaking and hoped she couldn't see it. "That's a California King."

"It's big." She chewed on her lip and stared at me. I gripped the footboard of my bed and leaned onto it. Layla crossed her legs under the blanket and pulled the comforter's corner back. "I'm not offering sex, but if you want to sleep beside me, I don't mind."

I nodded and pulled my shirt over my head. Layla's eyes widened as she took me in. It had been a few months since we went to the beach. Taking care of the ranch full-time added muscles in places the gym never came close to touching. I smirked, relishing her reaction, then stepped out of my jeans.

I slipped under the covers but didn't hug the edge of the bed. I took a spot near the center, closer to Layla, but not so close that I was pressuring her into anything. She rolled onto her side, adjusting herself so we were touching. I bit my tongue until I tasted blood, trying to distract my brain from her closeness with a surge of pain.

It worked until Layla turned toward me.

I looked down into her eyes, and after a moment of hesitation, she kissed me. I put my arm over her waist and pulled her closer, noticing how perfectly our bodies fit together. We stayed this way until Layla pushed my shoulder and rolled me onto my back. She climbed onto my lap, her kiss becoming more needy as her hands tugged at my hair.

And then she stopped.

Her eyes widened as if she was just realizing how much I wanted her. Or maybe, that she wanted me just as much. "I said no sex."

I chuckled and set my hands on her hips. "You're the one on top of me, gorgeous."

"Right." She turned her back to me and scooted to the far end of the bed. "Goodnight."

I kissed her shoulder and then tucked my hand behind my head. I probably shouldn't have let that kiss get so intense, but what could I say? I was a guy, and I enjoyed it.

I closed my eyes and felt my heartbeat pulse through my body. Tonight wasn't a total loss. Tomorrow would be even better. "Goodnight, beautiful."

My head was killing me. The curtains were drawn, and the blinds were closed, but it was still too bright. There was a reason I hadn't drank in over a year, and this pounding in my head was it. I covered my face with a pillow and squeezed my eyes shut.

Last night had been a disaster of epic proportions. I drank too much, had my mouth assaulted by Sam's tongue, and had the bomb of all bombs dropped on me.

Then, as if I wasn't confused enough, drunk-Layla had decided to climb on top of Josh and then freak out the moment his giant thing touched me. Through clothes! I was pathetic.

I peeked from underneath my pillow and noticed Josh was gone. Something in my chest tightened, and I feared he had decided to leave without saying goodbye. Then I remembered he had said he got up early to feed the horses. I pushed the panic aside and convinced myself there would be no walk of almost shame this morning.

Josh would be back, we would say a proper goodbye, and that would be that. I frowned, surprised at the wave of sadness that washed over me. As bad as last night had been, I didn't want to leave. I sat up, feeling the room move around me, and pressed my palm to my head.

After taking a minute to steady myself, I crawled out of bed and walked into the hallway. "Hello? Josh?"

He didn't answer. I stepped into the open living room-dining room-kitchen area and walked to the fridge. There was a bottle of cold water inside. I grabbed it and guzzled half of it in one breath. It helped, but my head still ached. I peeked through the window, looking out at more untouched grass than I'd ever seen in my life. There was no movement or anything to indicate Josh was around. I stepped to the front door and smiled when I opened it and saw his truck. He was still here.

I let out a breath I hadn't realized I was holding and headed back toward my room. Digging through my purse, I found two Tylenol in my emergency stash. After swallowing them down, I decided to explore the house, searching for a bathroom. I found it two doors down. There was a fresh set of towels on a rack above the toilet. I poked my head out the door one more time and figured, What the hell?

I stood under the shower's spray until the water lost its warmth. I hated a cold shower, so I got out and wrapped myself in a towel. Standing in front of the sink, I wiped my hand across the mirror. My eyes were still puffy from crying last night, but at least my headache was gone. I ran my fingers through my hair, then twisted my locks into a braid. Satisfied with what I saw, I decided it was time to get dressed and either head home or find Josh.

"Morning!" he shouted from one end of the hallway just as I walked out of the bathroom in a towel.

I jumped, and the thin terry cloth slipped out of my hand and fell to my feet. "Eek!" I squealed and bent down to re-cover myself, but the damage had been done. Josh had seen me naked and I had three-day stubble growing on my vag. Shoot me now.

"I have breakfast." He smirked. His eyes trailed down to my toes for a quick once-over, and my cheeks turned red.

"I'll... uh... I'll be ready in a minute." I hurried into Josh's room and shut the door behind me.

I fell onto the bed and covered my face with my arm. I had

thought about shaving before I left my house yesterday but reasoned that I wasn't getting naked, so it didn't matter. Had I known I'd be going commando this trip, I would have suffered through a day of razor burn to avoid the embarrassment.

Josh knocked at the door. I sat up, adjusting the towel around me, and noticed a huge wet spot on the sheets from my hair. I must have been lying there longer than I realized.

I opened the door and smiled. "What's up?"

"Everything okay here?"

"Yeah. I laid on the bed for a minute and lost track of time."

He smirked and heat climbed my neck to my cheeks again. These were the feelings I didn't know what to do with—this fluttering, heart-pumping, want-to-puke sensation that took over my thoughts and made it hard to function. "Have you ever been in a Gator?"

I shook my head, and the tiny hairs on the back of my neck stood on end. Josh didn't seem like the crazy redneck type. You know, the Joe Exotic kind of people that harbored illegal animals and found joy in feeding them food they weren't meant to have. I.e., me. "Please tell me you're not talking about the animal."

Josh sat in the driver's seat of an oversized four-wheeler. I'd been on a four-wheeler once and hated every minute of it. When I was sixteen, my brother Colson wanted to go to a Mud Festival. Mom and Dad never would have known we drove the four hours with his buddies if I hadn't broken my wrist. Needless to say, it wasn't the best experience, not to mention it was dirty. I wasn't a prissy girl, but washing a pound of mud out of my hair with a cast on my dominant hand was hell.

Josh offered me a small bottle of orange juice. I shook my head and struggled to look away from the beads of sweat dripping down his neck. Usually, I'd say guys who sweat were gross, but Josh pulled the look off. It probably helped that I knew he had gotten this way trying to do something nice for me.

At least, I hoped this ride would be nice.

"Are you ready?" he asked. I buckled myself in and nodded.

Josh grinned and put the side-by-side in gear. The engine was loud, almost like a motorcycle, but the music blaring through the speakers drowned it out. He drove around the back of his house and then floored it, slinging dirt behind him before peeling down a bumpy path.

"Are you good?" Josh yelled over the music. I tried to nod, but he hit a hole that sent me flying off my seat.

"Sorry." He slowed to half speed. "I'm excited to take you to the back forty. The only person who's been out there with me is Sam."

"It's cool." I cleared my throat and reached for the bottle of orange juice Josh tucked into a cup holder. I broke the seal and took a sip. Now that we were cruising, and I didn't have to worry about dying, this was kind of nice.

Josh put his arm over the back of the seat, and I unbuckled and scooted closer. My nerves ate at me with each second I wasn't strapped in. I trusted Josh, but it would take nothing to lose control.

He must have sensed my hesitation because he squeezed my hip and grinned. "I can run these roads with my eyes closed, beautiful."

"Roads?" I looked around at the untouched land that seemed to go on forever. "What roads?"

"There." Josh pointed to a path of pushed-down grass that was old enough to notice but new enough that I would have missed it if he hadn't shown it to me.

He hit a bump and I reached for his hand. I didn't mean to, but holding onto something made me feel safer. "Where I come from, roads are made of asphalt and sometimes dirt. But never grass."

"You're living in the wrong part of the world. This... it's a little piece of heaven."

I smacked my arm, killing a mosquito and spreading the blood it had tried to steal. "Your heaven is full of vampires."

Josh smirked and used the long sleeve of his shirt to wipe my arm. "Can you blame them for wanting to take a bite out of you?" His grin stretched wider. "Hang on to me."

I held Josh tight as he swerved into a puddle. Muddy water sprayed all over the windshield and splashed my legs. He spotted another puddle, this one the size of a tiny pool, and dove into it. It was maybe a foot deep, but at the speed we were going, there was enough water to splash up the sides of the Gator and sling mud everywhere.

Josh veered to the left, taking us down a dirt path and into the treeline. I huddled closer, a shiver slithering through me as the sun hid behind a veil of lush leaves. I closed my eyes, actually enjoying the ride. In a few hours, I had to return to Orlando and to my life. But for now, I could pretend nothing existed outside of this moment.

The sun emerged from behind the trees, and I opened my eyes again. Josh stopped the Gator at the shoreline of a large pond. He pulled his arm back without saying anything and walked toward the water as he tugged his shirt over his head. He was gorgeous. When he dropped his pants, I gulped.

"Josh... what are you doing?"

Walking backward into the water, he turned and said, "Swimming."

W ading waist-deep into the water, I got down on my knees and extended my arms. The coolness was heavenly against my hot skin. I dipped my head back, letting the water wash over my face. I wanted to take Layla horseback riding, but Maybelle hadn't been acting right the past few days, and Winston was too green to put her on. I wanted to ride the trial along the fence line so she could see the cows. It would have been romantic, but this was nice, too.

The pond in the back forty was big, stocked with bass that had been breeding since I was a boy. Paw and I used to come out here, just him and me, once a month and fish. He said it was important to carve out time for just the two of us and that the water had a way of grounding you. No matter how rough life got, we had it better than those fish. The only thing outside of the water for them was death, whereas I had the world at my feet—or so Paw had said.

I sat up again and wiped my hand over my face. Layla was peeling her shirt over her head. A second later, she slid her shorts down her hips and walked to the bank with her arms over her stomach.

"What are you doing?" I asked, unable to fathom why she would be insecure. The woman was gorgeous, but the crazy part was that she didn't even realize it. She had legs for days and a body most girls would kill for.

"Nothing." Layla's hands fell to her sides. I could tell she was uncomfortable, but she was trying to hide it, clenching her fist tighter, looser, and tighter again. If I hadn't seen that, I'd never have known.

I crept closer to the shore, keeping the water at my shoulders, anticipating her next move while failing miserably to slow my racing heartbeat. Layla walked to the edge and stuck out her right foot, dipping her toes into the water.

"Oh! It's cold!" she yelled, backtracking to the side-by-side.

I leapt up, the water only knee-deep now, and ran toward her. Layla stuck her arms out, shaking her hands at me as she walked backward a little faster. "No. No. No!"

She turned, breaking into a sprint as I reached the water's edge. I caught up to her and wrapped my arms around her waist while she screamed and laughed all at once. I bent down and grabbed her by the thighs, then threw her over my shoulders.

"Josh, no!" Layla flailed her legs and beat her fists against my back as I trekked back into the lake.

Water splashed up by my hips with each step until I was a little more than knee-deep. I peeled her off me and threw her a few feet away and into the water. A few seconds later, she stood and wiped her face with both hands, pushing her hair out of her eyes, which narrowed on me.

Layla walked to me at a snail's pace. The water was up to her waist, making it difficult for her to move with any speed. I held my ground, waiting for her to enact her revenge.

She did.

She lunged at me. Her chest pressed against mine, arms curling around my neck, while her legs wrapped around my waist. "That was mean."

I lowered us back into the water. Sitting like this, it was nearly to our shoulders. "I never said I was nice, beautiful."

She laced her fingers around my neck and shook her head.

"You're the nicest man I know, Josh, and I mean that in the best of ways."

My phone vibrated in the cup holder when we were almost back to the house. I pulled the side-by-side around the barn and washed the mud off before checking the message.

I must have frowned because Layla asked, "Is it that girl again? The one from Cowboy's?"

She tucked her hands in her back pockets and forced a smile, but I could feel it again—that tension from last night. It thickened with each millisecond I let hang between us and I wanted it gone.

"No." I tilted my phone so she could see the screen because I had nothing to hide. She needed to know that. "Sam's truck broke down again. He wants to know if I can come get him."

"You should go," she said, her shoulders not quite so tense.

"Are you sure?" I tossed my phone onto the side-by-side bench, then hooked my finger through Layla's belt loop. I pulled her closer, until we were toe to toe.

Layla tucked her hair behind her ear and grinned, that beautiful flush of pink covering her cheeks again. "I should be heading home anyway. I know you wanted me to stay the week-end, but I've got to get a hold of some donors for my next event."

I didn't want her to go, but I understood. My job was my life and I respected that hers was, too. Most people our age didn't have a good work ethic. "I want to see you again."

"Oh, you do?" She smirked and set her hands on my chest.

I tilted my head down until our foreheads touched. I didn't care what it took, and I didn't care that an attraction this strong didn't make sense. I needed this woman in my life. "I do."

She pressed a chaste kiss to my lips, then pushed me back, a playful grin in place. "I'm leaving before I give in to whatever this is."

"Okay," I said through a chuckle, fully understanding what she meant. "Let me walk you to the house to get your things."

"No!" Layla held her hand out to me. "You stay there." I looked at her curiously, and she added, "This is hard, Josh. I want to stay. I want to kiss you and..." Her cheeks flushed red again and she bit her lip. "You make me want to do things I've only read about in books, which scares me. So, you stay right where you are. That way, when I get into my car, I'll stay there and not run back across this grass and rip your shirt off."

Josh: What are you doing on Saturday?

My earbud read the text message as I folded the linens from last week's event. Even though I had been working hard to keep my grades up this semester, I was still working for my aunt. Part-time, of course, and for the same pathetic excuse of a salary, but money was money.

I never realized how expensive food was. Or gas, for that matter. It cost me sixty dollars every time I visited Josh. And while I had only been there three times since school started, that was almost a quarter of my monthly allowance. I set the clean tablecloth in a plastic tub along with the others from last week's event and swiped my phone off the table.

Me: My brother and his buddies are flying into Orlando for a guy's weekend. I was going to hang with them on Saturday. 😕

Josh: That blows. Bret and I are going to be at City Walk.

Me: I'm sorry 😢

Josh: You're killing me. I miss you.

Me: You do?

Josh: Yeah. This weekend wasn't the same
without you.

Me: You're sweet.

Josh: Not sweet. Just honest.

The rest of the day dragged. I finished putting away the linens, organized the vases in our decor closet, and hand-wrote forty thank-you cards, all while waiting for Josh to text me again.

He didn't, and as I collapsed onto the twin mattress in my studio apartment, I couldn't shake the feeling of disappointment. We had fallen into a routine of sorts, texting during the week and hanging out on the ranch on the weekends. But Aunt Tricia had an event last Saturday, so I couldn't drive down.

I grabbed my phone from beside my pillow and hit the video chat app. We had never talked like this, but the ache I had in the pit of my stomach to see him was too strong.

The screen rang three times before Josh answered. He squinted against the sun, the shadow of his hand around the camera as he tried to see me on the screen. "Layla?"

"Is this a bad time?" Of course, it was a bad time. He was probably working on the farm, milking a cow or something. Outside of feeding the horses, I didn't know what Josh did for a living.

"No, it's fine. Hang on a sec." Josh set his phone on the grass, and I could see him pulling off a pair of gloves. He dropped them to the ground and then picked me back up. "Hey."

"What were you doing?"

"Fixing the fence. Last night, some kids cut the wire to ride through on their four-wheelers." He turned the camera around so

I could see the tire tracks and a roll of barbed wire he was tacking to the wooden posts. "They only cut one section, which isn't bad, but it still sucks. I got lucky the cows were on the other half of the field."

"I'm sorry." I rolled to sit cross-legged and propped my phone against the pillow.

My heart raced in my chest, and suddenly, it was too hot in there. The flowy blouse and tank top I had worn all day squeezed my chest like a vice. I swallowed the knot in my throat and tried to focus on our conversation. It was hard, though, with beads of sweat dripping down Josh's brow. He raised his muscular, tan arm and wiped the droplets away.

"Does that happen often?"

Josh smirked and shook his head. "Nah, maybe twice a year. How was your day?"

"Mine?" I pulled my overshirt off as he shifted to sit in the shade of the side-by-side. I lay on my belly, the tight tank and my push-up bra making my girls look fantastic from this angle, and then grabbed my phone again. "It was boring. I had to put everything we used at the event last weekend away, catalog it to ensure nothing was lost, then handwrite thank-you notes."

"Sounds tedious."

"You have no idea."

We stared at each other, neither of us knowing what to say for a minute. The silence was awkward and heavy. I wished I were back in Fellsmere with him, but it would be almost nine by the time I got through rush hour traffic and made my way there. If I didn't have an eight a.m. class, I'd probably go. I could stay the night and curl up in his arms again, but I couldn't risk morning traffic making me late, and there was no point in driving all that way to stay for only an hour.

"I've got to finish up before the sun goes down," he finally said, rising to his feet.

I forced a smile because, as much as I didn't want to admit it, I missed Josh. Despite the hiccup at Cowboy's a few weeks ago, I had a great time with him, and the two other times I had gone back had been even better than the one before.

I'd probably meet Josh and his brother at City Walk if Colson weren't coming to town. I hadn't been there yet, but some girls I worked with said it was a blast. "Right, of course."

"Hey, Layla?"

"Yeah?"

"Thanks for calling. I'm glad I got to see your face."

A swarm of butterflies flurried inside me. I couldn't explain it. I had never felt anything so crazy, wonderful, and terrifying all at once. "Bye, Josh."

"Goodbye, beautiful."

"There's my baby sister!" Colson held his arms out and swooped me into a hug, rocking me from side to side.

The embrace was awkward. We weren't a lovey family. Growing up, the best we could hope for from our parents was a nod of approval and, if we were lucky, words of praise. With that as our model, Cole and I had shaken hands a total of four times. As for hugs, this was a first.

Cole pulled back just as the hug went from awkward to uncomfortable and I smelled vodka on his breath. It wasn't a subtle hint, either. He reeked of it, like the plane had a pool filled with it and he went swimming. "Are you drunk?"

"Is there any other way to be on a guy's weekend?" Ashley, my ex-boyfriend, inquired. He stood in the middle of a group of Cole's friends, guys I recognized but didn't know by name.

I schooled my face, forcing the discomfort of being around him again behind a pleasant smile. Breaking off our wedding had been the best decision I'd ever made, but I'd be lying if I said the feelings were mutual.

Ashley might have been a conniving, cheating scumbag, but for some reason, he didn't want to let me go. He never loved me, so I assumed it was a possession thing. I was supposed to be his and the thought of me being with someone else irked him.

But I couldn't do it. Not after I had caught Sharon Deese, a waitress at the country club, on her knees in the girl's bathroom. Ashley had smirked when I found them, likely wanting me to see a glimpse of our future. I would have puked right there, but was in my bathroom. The one space that was supposed to be a sanctuary in life, and he'd invaded it.

I had run out with tears brewing in my eyes and slammed into my mother. I had told her what I'd seen and begged her to call off the marriage.

Her reaction?

She popped a Prozac from the tiny bottle that lived in every purse she owned and chased it with her vodka tonic, saying, "We marry for power, not for love, chickpea. Ashley will have his indiscretions, and so will you. Dry your eyes and come back to the table with a smile."

That day I decided to forge my own future. I wouldn't be a pawn in my parents' business and I wasn't going to marry that pig.

"You would encourage this unbecoming behavior." I rolled my eyes at Ashley and smoothed the invisible wrinkles on my dress. I walked beside my brother to baggage claim, trying my hardest to ignore my ex. "What's the plan for this weekend?"

"Boobs and booze." Ashley smirked, knowing he was working my last nerve. He raised his hand and one of the guys high-fived him.

I scrunched my nose and shook my head. I could care less what Ashley did or with whom, but I'd rather claw my eyes out with one of those plastic spoon-fork combo utensils than spend the weekend at a strip club watching girls fawn over my brother. "That sounds…"

Horrible.

Atrocious.

Like a living nightmare.

"Relax." Cole chuckled and threw his arm over my shoulder. "That's tomorrow. Tonight is your night, little sister. We're going to hit up City Walk, drink, dance, and listen to music."

I perked up at the possibility of running into Josh tonight. Cole probably wouldn't like that I was hanging out with someone of the opposite sex, and there was a chance Ashley would go full-on douchebag, but I didn't care. After an hour or so with the guys, I could text Josh to see if he wanted to meet up.

"What are you smiling at?" Ashley asked in his all-too-familiar, demanding tone.

I ignored him and pulled out my phone to search for what City Walk had to offer. Tonight might actually be fun.

WE SQUISHED around a table meant for four. Colson sat on one side of me, his arm thrown over my chair, and Ashley on the other. The guys, whose names I had picked up as being Jackson, Ambrose, Chris, and Austin, pulled chairs from surrounding tables to sit with us.

Colson chugged another beer, his eighth one since arriving at this bar, and stood. He walked to one of the Piano Guys at the front of the room, dropped a few bills into the jar, and then handed over another song request. Instead of returning to the table, Colson stumbled toward the back of the establishment, likely to the bathroom.

I watched him, unease simmering inside me. Something was going on. I had never seen Colson drunk before. Tipsy, yes, but he was hitting a new level tonight.

Two songs played, but Colson still hadn't returned to the table. I peeked around the room and decided to wait for him by the bathrooms since he wasn't anywhere in sight.

After ten minutes of standing in the hallway near the restrooms, I was shaking with nervous energy. Colson was drunk, really drunk. He could be passed out on the bathroom floor and his buddies wouldn't notice, let alone care.

I waited until another song ended, then decided I was going in. No one had gone in or out of the men's bathroom for at least two songs. I reached for the handle, but a figure coming down the hall caused me to hesitate. I frowned, recognizing the man, and crossed my arms. "It's about time."

"Why? Have you been waiting for me?" Ashley chuckled and grabbed my wrists, pulling me into him. I had kept my distance as much as I could tonight, but this close I was choking on his cologne.

"Ew. No." I pressed my palms against his chest to add some space between us, but he laughed and held me tighter. "I'm worried about Colson. You should go into the bathroom and check on him."

Ashley dipped his mouth to my neck and bile crept up my throat. All I could think about was that girl. The memory of him with his hands behind his head as she bobbed up and down on her knees was etched into my brain. It made me sick, physically sick.

"Colson is back at the table." Ashley sank his teeth into my skin. He bit down like a drunk vampire, pressing too hard in all the wrong places.

I tilted my head, pinching my shoulder up, and pushed against Ashley's chest again, but he wasn't getting the picture. "Stop it."

An unwelcome hand fell to my thigh and slipped underneath my dress. I gripped Ashley's wrist and pushed it away, but it was back on my inner thigh before I could take a solid breath.

Fear ignited in my veins. Ashley was drunk and not used to being told no. I stepped my defense up and grabbed his hair to yank his mouth off my skin. "I said stop!"

Flames danced behind a cloudy haze in Ashley's eyes. He slammed me against the wall, and his lips assaulted mine. I bit his tongue as soon as it pushed between my teeth.

Ashley grunted and reared back. He didn't hesitate before slapping me across the face. "You fucking bitch!"

For a moment, I was stunned. Ashley may have been insensitive and unfaithful, but he was never abusive. I reached up and touched my cheek. The sting of his hand lingered, but it was nothing compared to the pain pooling in my eyes. *I will not cry.*

"Hey!" Josh's voice boomed from behind me and I'd never been so relieved to see him. He stormed up to us, grabbed Ashley by the shirt collar, and then pushed him up against the wall.

Ashley chuckled, too drunk to realize that things for him had taken a turn for the worse. "What the hell do you think you're doing?"

Josh slammed Ashley's back against the wall again. Colson ran into the room two minutes too late and gripped the back of Josh's shirt. He pulled Josh backward and extended his arms between the two to keep them separated.

Josh puffed his chest and the man, I assume to be his brother, clapped a hand on Josh's shoulder. He exhaled heavily, then crossed his arms and glared at his brother before refocusing on Ashley.

"Layla?" Colson asked, his hooded gaze fixating on me before bouncing to his friend and the two boys behind me. "Are you okay?"

"She's fine," Ashley answered. He reached for my arm, but I twisted and moved to stand beside Josh.

The thought of Ashley touching me again made me tremble. I crossed my arms, holding them tight against my chest, and dug my nails into my sides. *Everything will be alright.*

"You must be Layla's brother. I'm Josh." If these were better circumstances, I think Josh would extend his hand. However, they stayed clenched beside his body.

Colson arched a brow, unimpressed. "And I care because?"

I didn't think about my next words. They flowed like a faucet and were out of me before I could take them back.

Maybe it was because I wanted Josh to be my boyfriend, or maybe I wanted Ashley to back off. Either way, the damage was done when I said, "Because he's my boyfriend."

Josh wrapped his arm around my waist and pulled me close without missing a beat. He turned his gaze to Ashley, staring him down. "And you are?"

"The fiancé."

"Ex-fiancé," I added. Outside of a vague conversation back in March, I purposely avoided anything Ashley-related. I didn't think it mattered because we weren't together anymore. Josh had a past before me that I've never asked about, and that door went both ways.

"Semantics, my love."

"Last I checked, ex means you aren't together," Josh's brother, Bret, interjected.

"I don't know what is going on." Colson paused to look at Josh and Bret. "Or why you two are here, but if it's all the same to you, I'd like to spend time with my sister."

Ashley smirked and sauntered back into the lounge. I shuddered, feeling phantom lips on my neck, and rubbed the saliva away. "I can't. I'm sorry, Colson, but I don't trust Ashley."

"You're his fiancée, Layla. If he wants to touch you, he can. It's his right."

My jaw dropped at the realization that he saw everything. Colson saw me struggle to push Ashley away, probably heard me yelling "No," and he did nothing.

Ashley violated me with his mouth and would have with his hand if Josh hadn't shown up. Just because we used to be engaged didn't make it okay. Together or not, when a girl said stop, you stopped.

Cole didn't even acknowledge me. He acted as if he hadn't heard me at all.

"He lost the right to do anything with me when he cheated. Besides, Mom and Dad agreed that I didn't have to marry Ashley so long as I was in school."

Colson snorted and looked at me like I was nothing more than his ignorant kid sister. "You won't be in school forever. What did you think would happen when you came back?"

I shook my head, tears pooling in my eyes again. The knot in the pit of my stomach that I lived with since I was thirteen returns. The one that told me I was trapped and there was nothing I could do about my situation. Only, I wasn't a kid anymore and there's no way in hell I was giving up my freedom.

"I'm not coming back, Colson." I wanted to yell, but wars weren't won with emotions. This fight would be over, with me deemed *impossible,* the moment I lost control. "Things aren't as easy for me as they are for you."

"You think I have it easy? You're delusional, Layla." Colson shook his head and turned his back to me. "But fine. If you'd rather slum it up with these assholes, then be my guest."

My heart told me to chase after my brother, that leaving now would do more damage to us than good, but my gut warned me not to stay.

Ashley had been drunk, with an agenda Colson agreed with. If I had stayed, there was a good chance Ashley would have come onto me again, and I doubted he would have stopped at kissing.

"So, you're Layla." Bret held out his hand. "I'm Bret, Josh's brother."

I forced a smile. I was happy to meet him, but I wished it was under better circumstances. I shook his hand and then curled back into Josh's side. "The one and only."

Bret smirked and held the door open. I exited first, with Josh close behind me. He was back at my hip the moment we were outside, a protective arm around me. We walked silently away from the Piano Bar and the weight of what had gone down crushed me.

My brother was willing to let Ashley have his way with me.

He had defended his best friend, not his sister.

It was a betrayal that hurt more than I could have imagined, even if I should have expected it.

"You know, I'm going to be a doctor soon." Bret winked and I didn't know what to do besides laugh. This—him hitting on me—was exactly what I had expected after hearing the rumors. Supposedly, girls lined up to have their hearts broken, but I got the feeling Bret was trying to make me feel better rather than steal me away from his brother.

Josh shoved him in the shoulder, either unaware or not caring that the line had been a joke. Bret chuckled and shook his head, ignoring Josh as he said, "Shut up, you idiot."

I forced another smile. My heart was heavy. Despite my brother acting like a jerk, I was worried about Colson and wondered why he was drinking so much. I worried his friends wouldn't take care of him. Most of all, I worried I ruined the fragile relationship he and I had forged.

"I'm sorry I ruined your night," I said as we headed toward the front entrance of City Walk.

Colorful lights illuminated the sidewalk, creating a haze that hid the stars in the night sky. Even though the theme parks had closed hours ago, people still bustled from one bar to the next, making the sidewalks just as crowded as they were during the day.

"Hijacked, yeah," Bret teased. "But not ruined. I'd rather look at you than this clown any day."

Josh flipped Bret the middle finger and then kissed my temple. He hadn't let me go for more than a minute since we had left the Piano Bar. I was grateful. If left to my own devices, I probably would have been curled up in some corner, crying.

Josh eyed me, noticing the subtle downturn of my lips, and asked, "Are you sure you're all right?"

I forced yet another smile and tried to believe my own words. "Yeah, a little shaken up, but I'm good. Ashley wouldn't have..."

Josh pressed his lips to my temple and I lost all train of thought. I was okay with that. I'd rather not think about Ashley and what could have happened had Josh not shown up when he did.

Bret glanced at his watch and yawned. "It's getting late. Do you want to call it a night?"

"Yes." Josh gave his brother a look, probably having a silent conversation, then faced me. "How are you getting home?"

"I…" I had ridden in the limo with Colson, but I didn't want to be near Ashley. I couldn't afford a cab, but my car was at their hotel. I pushed my long bangs back and took a deep breath. "I don't know."

"Tell you what. Bret…" Josh fished in his pocket for his keys and tossed them at his brother. "Take the truck or leave it if you don't feel up to driving."

Bret snickered and arched his eyebrows. "Seriously, bro? I taught you how to drive."

"Hey, man, you could have gone soft under those city lights. I'm going to grab an Uber and see Layla home."

"Sounds good."

They hugged, and Bret gave Josh a knowing smirk. He shook his head and grinned. "Lovely to meet you, Layla."

"Hey, Josh?" I asked as we rode the elevator to my apartment. I was on the third floor, wedged between a hard-rock-loving grandpa and a single mom of three rowdy kids under the age of five. The walls were paper thin, but I wouldn't have had it any other way. Hearing their lives through the walls (even if it seemed creepy) made me feel like I wasn't alone.

"Yeah?"

I stopped in front of my door, number 309, and chewed on my bottom lip. As much as I had wanted to see him, it was safe to say tonight hadn't gone as planned.

"Would you mind staying? The guys all know where I live and I don't trust Ashley not to show up tonight."

"Yeah, of course." He smiled, and I nodded, all too aware of what my home looked like compared to his.

Hattie's cottage only felt tiny because it was always packed with people. My efficiency felt small because it was small. I flipped the light on as I opened the door.

"This is nice," he said as soon as he stepped inside.

I dropped my keys in the ceramic pumpkin on my kitchen counter and forced myself to breathe. My hands shook. I tucked them behind me and leaned against the dishwasher. "It's small."

Josh turned and took my elbow. He pulled me into him and held me close. "No one ever said small wasn't nice."

I shrugged and left his arms, stepping deeper into my five-hundred-square-foot home. "So, that's the bed. There's a bathroom through there. I... um... I have some cereal and a few things if you're hungry."

"I'm good." Josh sat on my mattress and began to unlace his boots. He kicked one off and then the other before shrugging out of his pants.

"Just so we're clear. I know I asked you to stay, but I'm not having sex with you."

"You know," he pulled the comforter on my twin bed back and scooted close to the wall, "if I wasn't so sure of myself, I might be offended, considering you've felt the need to say that twice now."

I rolled my eyes, feigning confidence, and unzipped my dress. Josh had seen me naked. Once. On accident. But standing in front of him in nothing but my black lace bra and matching panties was nerve-racking.

Josh stared at me, a slight smirk on his face, refusing to look away. I sauntered over to the four-drawer dresser my TV sat on and grabbed a silk nightie from the top drawer. I faced the wall and unclasped my bra. It fell to my feet. I sucked in a breath, feeling Josh's eyes on my back, then slipped the nightgown on.

Josh cleared his throat. "Why... uh... why do you keep saying that?"

I turned toward him and twisted my hair into a braid.

Sitting on the edge of my bed, I wondered how we would both fit here tonight, but I figured if Landon and Hattie could make a twin-sized bed work, Josh and I could, too.

"Because I don't trust myself around you. We might get carried away if I don't put it out there. If I say it, you'll stop before things go too far."

I laid on my side, our faces inches from each other. Josh pulled the cover over us and draped his arm across my hip. "How do you know?"

"Because I trust you." I pressed my lips to his and cupped Josh's cheek.

We'd been doing this for a few weeks now, kissing and sleeping beside each other, and Josh had never asked for more. He never pressured me into something I wasn't ready for, but I could feel how much he wanted me.

And as crazy as it was, considering the night I had, I wanted him too.

I took his hand, put it between my legs, and whispered, "I want you to touch me."

"Are you sure?" he asked, and I nodded.

His hand slid under my panties, and all the air was pulled from my lungs the second I felt his fingers. I couldn't move, couldn't think, because what he was doing hurt but felt good, too.

"Is this okay?"

I nodded and found my breath again, only to lose it when the first orgasm I'd had in months hit me. I fell into the sensation and when it passed I reached for Josh's pants, wanting to make him feel just as good, but he grunted and pulled his hand away.

He pressed his forehead against mine and exhaled heavily. "We should stop."

"We don't have to," I said meekly.

"When the day comes that you don't start the night by

saying you don't want sex, we'll do more. Until then, this is me doing my best to respect your wishes." He pressed his lips against mine for a quick kiss.

I nodded and closed my eyes, feeling the weight of sleep coming over me until Josh spoke again. "What are you doing for Thanksgiving?"

"I'm supposed to fly back home. No one's asked me to, but it's been implied, especially since Aunt Tricia is going."

Josh ran his fingers down my back, trailing lazy circles. "You don't want to?"

"Ashley's family is bound to be there. You saw what he's like."

"So, you're just going to what? Stay here by yourself?"

"It beats going home and dealing with that mess." I rolled onto my back and stared at my ceiling, making constellations out of tiny popcorn pieces.

The first night I moved in, I couldn't sleep. I stayed up for hours, counting each speck until eventually nodding off. I had no interest in counting specks tonight. I just couldn't look at him right now.

"I'm not marrying Ashley. I told my parents that, but they seem to think I'll change my mind and come crawling back. The longer I stay away, the better off I am."

Josh cupped my cheek and forced me to look at him. "You should have Thanksgiving at my house."

My stomach somersaulted. Holidays and meeting the parents were significant steps in a relationship, and we were... Well, I don't know what we were. "That's still a few weeks out."

"What can I say?" He smirked. "I'm locking you in."

"I don't know, Josh." I wanted him to ask me to be his. I wanted things between us to jump to the next step, but I didn't want to ruin the good thing we had going by adding the pressure of a label.

"What if you were my girlfriend? Would you come then?

I've wanted to say something for a while now, but It didn't seem like a conversation that should be done through a text. So, what do you say, Layla? Be my girl?"

I wanted this, but a tiny voice in my mind threw darts laced with doubt at my heart. "We live two hours apart. How do you expect this to work?"

"Same as it has been. We'll see each other every weekend, with either you coming down or me driving up to see you. We'll text during the day and FaceTime at night."

I shook my head, still unsure about a long-distance relationship. Ashley was unfaithful and he lived five minutes away. Two hours apart... anything could happen.

"You could have any girl, Josh. Why me? My family is a level of crazy you can't begin to understand. I'm in school and still working, so my time is going to be monopolized. You should..."

He silenced me with a searing kiss. One that made me forget all of my doubts for a minute. I wanted this. I shouldn't fight it, but I was scared.

"Nothing in life worth having is easy. What's the worst that'll happen?"

I fall too hard and you break my heart?

"Say yes. Please?"

"Alright, Josh. Yes."

"**G**irl." Hattie plopped onto the couch beside me. Her living room was tiny, but because of the open concept, having five people crammed into it didn't feel so bad. It helped that the guys were on the floor, playing some video game where they shot each other. "What are you wearing for the Halloween party tonight?"

"I thought Halloween was on Monday."

"You would know that." Hattie rolled her eyes and took a sip of her lemonade. "Well, we can't party on a weeknight. Now, can we?"

I shrugged and picked at the fries left in my takeout bag. There wasn't much left, but thinking about the holidays made me nervous. Even though Halloween wasn't one I was expected to call home about, it meant Thanksgiving was around the corner, and then Christmas. My parents would have my head if I didn't attend at least one. Not to mention, with holidays came gifts, and I couldn't exactly afford to be handing money out like that. I grabbed another fry, then frowned when I realized there were no more.

"Are you hungry?" Hattie arched a brow at me. I shook my head and dropped the empty cardboard container into my bag. She looked at me a moment longer, then said, "So, I was thinking we should have a theme."

"Isn't dressing up a little... I don't know, high schoolish?"

That was a stretch, in my opinion. The last time I put on a costume, let alone did anything for Halloween, I was twelve.

"First of all, I'll pretend like you started that sentence with no offense. Secondly..." Hattie grabbed the throw pillow beside her and whacked Josh on the head.

"Dude?" Josh looked away from the screen long enough for Hattie to smirk, and someone in the game killed his avatar. "Damnit, Hattie. That was my last life."

"Well, maybe if you spent more time here and not on that stupid farm, you wouldn't suck so bad." She crossed her arms and smirked as if her statement was supposed to hurt Josh's feelings. Only I knew that despite its hardships, Josh loved what he did.

"Yeah, because getting high and playing games all day will pay my bills." He climbed off the floor and wiggled between Hattie and me on the couch. "I'm good."

"Have you thought about your costume for the party?"

Josh put his arm around my shoulder and pulled me close. I rested my head on his chest, feeling that heat build inside me again. It had been a week since we officially started dating.

"Layla and I are doing the *Blue Lagoon* thing. You know her in a fringe skirt, hair covering her tits, and me with my wang out."

"Wait, what?" I stared at Josh, waiting for him to tell me he was joking, but he was straight-faced, looking at the screen.

All of a sudden, he laughed and shook his head. "No, I haven't thought about my costume. There are more important things on my mind than that."

"We should go shopping together!" Hattie squealed and jumped off the couch. She walked over to the TV and pushed the power button, earning a few choice words from Landon and Sam that she chose to ignore. "Up. We are heading into town."

Josh

Of all the holidays, today was my least favorite. My uncle had a heart attack while working at the haunted house St. Anastasia's hosted every year. Everyone assumed he was a prop, or someone who would grab your ankle, but he wasn't. He laid there for eight hours before Mom called the police and reported him missing.

It's why I hate Halloween.

"Raaar!" Hattie yelled, jumping from behind a costume display with a T-Rex mask over her head.

I forced a smile and playfully shoved her shoulder. She wasn't around when my uncle died, and even though my friends were, they forgot how hard today was. I grabbed a top hat I had no intention of buying and set it on my head.

"Anything catch your eye?" I asked Layla.

She stared at a wall of costumes, nibbling on her bottom lip. She shook her head and frowned. "Everything is out of my price range and their clearance section sucks."

"Well, since you won't let me pay for your gas..." I offered every weekend Layla drove down. I knew she was on a strict budget, which was why we didn't go out or if we did, I paid. Although she griped about that, too. "The least you can let me do is buy your costume so we can match."

"I don't want your money, Josh."

"I know." I took Layla by the wrist and pulled her into me. I'd held more girls than I cared to admit, kissed them, tasted their most intimate parts, but they never made me feel the way Layla did. "but I'd be a horrible boyfriend if I didn't spoil my girl."

"That's right. I forgot you were my boyfriend." She smirked, and I knew she was playing. I didn't bother fighting my smile or falling into her trap.

"Did you? I should remind you then." I dipped my head and

pressed my lips to hers. Kissing Layla was like breathing: easy, yet necessary to survive.

It killed me to watch her pull out of my driveway every Sunday. I usually stood there, waving with a smile on my face, while the Tasmanian Devil berated my insides with a sledgehammer.

Every minute we were apart felt like a lifetime in itself. So, I threw myself into the farm, waking at four and working until I was close to passing out. The last thing I wanted was a rumor about me being at a party to drive a wedge between us.

Small towns brought big drama.

My phone dinged in my pocket. I pulled away from Layla's lips with a grunt and rested my forehead against hers. I didn't want to look at the message. The only person I cared to talk to was in my arms.

"Are you going get that?" Layla whispered.

I opened my eyes and she looked up at me, her lips lifting in the corners. She teased me with one more kiss before pulling back again. I was barely able to take a breath before Hattie pulled her by the hand to another part of the store.

I sighed, dreading tonight's party, and looked at my phone. I wished I hadn't.

Amanda: There's something wrong with the baby.

Amanda: One of the tests came back wonky. They think he might have something wrong with his spine.

Amanda: I'm so scared, Josh.

Me: I'm sorry. That sucks.

Amanda: Really? That's all you have to say.

Me: Yeah. I'm sorry your kid isn't growing right, but he's not mine.

Amanda: Seriously! Bryson is your son. I wasn't sleeping with anyone else!

Me: I'll believe that when I see it. Either way, I hope your baby is okay.

"Hey!" Layla wrinkled her brows when she turned the corner, her smile falling. "Everything alright?"

"Yeah." I shut my phone off. Amanda may have been having a rough time, but I didn't need to be dragged into her problems. She had a family and a baby daddy out there who should've been helping her through this. Not me. I gestured at the costume packs Layla hugged to her chest. "Find something you like?"

"Maybe." She smirked and I got this feeling tonight was about to get interesting. "Promise you'll keep an open mind. Okay?"

Giving Layla shots may have been a bad idea. That girl was the epitome of white-girl wasted, but she was adorable. Her hips swayed from right to left, the flap of her cowgirl dress creeping dangerously high with each movement.

Hattie's idea of group costumes had lasted about as long as Landon did in bed—two minutes—before his shirt came off.

Hattie was dressed as a sexy cop who had caught her fugitive. Sam was a vampire intent on leaving his mark on as many girls as would let him. As for Layla, she had wanted to braid her hair and be a cowgirl and had wanted me to be her cowboy, but she wouldn't let me wear my work clothes. She had wanted me in fringe chaps, a faux leather vest, and holsters with toy guns. I thought it was lame, but she compromised and agreed I could wear my hat.

I took Layla by the hand, spun her once, and then pulled her into me. She laughed, tripped over her feet, and fell against my chest.

"I don't know how you walk in boots every day," she mumbled, her cheeks flushed red. Hattie's fringe boots were two sizes too big for Layla's tiny feet, but she insisted on wearing them because they matched the costume.

"It helps if they're the right size." I swayed Layla's hips, seamlessly taking us from standing to dancing as the song changed into something slower. "I'm of a fan of them on you."

"Really? Because I'm a fan of you right now."

"Careful. If you keep talking like this, people will think you like me." I leaned down and pressed my mouth to hers. Layla tasted like strawberry Jell-O, likely from the shots she pounded back.

"Let them." Her breath hitched when my lips grazed the crook of her neck at the sweet spot that made her squirm.

Hands that had just been at my hips gripped the sides of my shirt. My lips moved up her neck, leaving a pathway of kisses behind them.

But like usual, she took a step back when she felt like she was losing control, putting too many inches between us. "I...uhh... I'm going to go to the bathroom."

I twirled a strand of fringe that covered her chest around my finger. "Want me to come with you?"

"Yes." She smirked, walking backward as she said, "But I need to pee. Not exactly sexy."

"Everything you do is sexy," I told her and it wasn't a line.

Layla shook her head and blushed. "Only you, Joshua Thomas. Only you."

I stared at the stars from one of the six folding chairs surrounding Landon's makeshift fire pit. Empty beer boxes burned on top of logs, crackling in the warm fall air. My lips twitched, curving into a smile as I sipped my soda. For the first time in years, I didn't hate Halloween.

"I thought I'd find you out here." Amanda took the chair beside me, dressed like a scarecrow with a pumpkin over the beginnings of a bump. She was all belly, although there wasn't much belly to be. She was so tiny, it was scary.

"What do you want?" I refused to look at her, instead

crossing my arms behind my head and scooting down in my chair until I was comfortable.

"The doctor said Bryson's spine looked good. He thinks the lab made an error on my test but doesn't feel comfortable returning me to my OB. Apparently, I'm considered high risk now."

"I'm glad your baby is okay." I was. I might not have cared about Amanda or the kid, but no one wanted to hear their baby had an abnormality. As a parent, you dealt with whatever you were given and loved the kid no matter what... but still.

"Our baby, Josh." Amanda shifted in her chair and stared at me until I gave in and looked at her. "Bryson is our baby. Why won't you admit it?"

"Because he's not my kid." Plain and simple. If the condom had broken, I might have been worried, but like I said, the odds of him being mine were slim to none.

"If you're worried about that tramp you've been screwing the last few weeks, I took care of her," Amanda said so matter-of-factly I was shaken. There was no malice in her tone or even bitterness.

She sounded almost remorseful, which was why I wasn't yelling. I was confused. "What are you talking about?"

"Lula, or whatever her name is, isn't going to come between us anymore." Amanda reached out and set her hand on my arm. "She knows and understands."

I stood and shook Amanda's hand off me. I scanned the backyard but didn't see Layla anywhere. There was a chance she was in the house somewhere, but I had a gut feeling something was wrong. "What the hell did you say to her?"

"The truth!" Amanda yelled, pushing out of her chair. "I told her that once Bryson is born, we're getting married."

"Have you lost your mind?" I ran my hands through my hair and looked at the sky again. This woman was pushing my last nerve.

"I won't raise our baby in a broken home, Josh. Not happening." She set her hands on her hips and shot me a look that I think was supposed to make me nervous.

I was nervous. Nervous Amanda might have screwed up the best thing to happen to me. I ran toward the house, leaving Amanda and her pleas to talk behind me.

That baby wasn't mine, but even if it were, I still wouldn't marry her. I refused to trap myself in a loveless marriage and raise a kid in a toxic environment.

What the hell was I thinking? It wasn't mine. I didn't need to worry about that.

I yanked the door to Hattie's cottage open and ran inside. Only a few people were in the livingroom, but none were Layla. I crossed the tiny house in quick strides and reached for the bedroom handle. It was locked, as expected, and I didn't have my keys.

I ran out the door again and across the field to the church parking lot. I had given Layla my key ring when she had to go to the bathroom. I didn't think she would drive drunk—she seemed smarter than that—but people did stupid things when upset. Considering how badly things had gone the last time Amanda showed up, I'd say tonight was about to spiral downward.

I let out a breath I didn't know I had been holding when I saw Layla sitting on my toolbox, staring up at the sky. My keys were beside her, along with a bottle of water and her cell phone.

"I texted you a few minutes ago," she said, turning her head to me when I leaned against the side of the truck. "I don't feel much like partying anymore."

"Amanda's a bitch. You can't listen to a word she says."

"She's not a bitch, Josh. She's scared. I know you say that baby isn't yours, but she's holding on to a shred of hope that it is." Layla sighed and looked up at the stars again. "Are you going to marry her?"

"Hell, no." I dropped the tailgate and climbed onto the bed to sit beside her. "On the off chance that kid is mine—which it's not—I don't love her. Having a kid isn't a reason to get married."

Layla bit her lip, probably reading too deeply into what I said. I didn't love Layla, but I could one day. I liked her enough, but it was too soon to cross that bridge.

"My parents don't love each other. They don't even like one another,' she said softly.

I cupped Layla's cheek and forced her to look at me. "That won't be me. My mother loved my dad so much that she never married again after he left us. I want a love like that. I want to be with someone who makes my heart race so fast it skips a beat. I want to wake up with that person every day and know that, no matter what, we've got each other's back. I want that person to be my best friend because being a partner isn't good enough. Amanda can never be that person to me."

Layla was quiet for a long time. I needed her to speak. I was going crazy in my head. Given enough time, she could be that person. What we had was special. She had got to know that. I didn't want to lose her because of some crazy pregnant chick.

"Those are some big shoes to fill."

I smiled, relieved that she might want to fill them. "That's why I haven't dated in years. I never met anyone I thought was right for the job."

"And you think I am?"

"I think you could be." My hand slid from Layla's cheek to the base of her neck. I wanted to kiss her and feel her body mold against mine. To hold her soft curves and let the fire that comes with her touch consume me.

But Layla pulled back. I laid my heart out there for nothing. My stomach dropped to my feet. I didn't bother to hide the downturn of my lips. Layla didn't break my heart. I may have been falling for the girl, but I wasn't that deep. She just put a chip in it that ached and reminded me why I didn't put myself out there anymore.

"Take me home, Josh." She stood and hopped off the tailgate. "Because I'd hate for our first time to be in a church parking lot."

I didn't expect that. My lips twitched, turning upward. "It would make a great story for our grandkids one day."

Layla smirked. "Don't get ahead of yourself. If you don't have the moves, there won't be any grandkids."

"Oh, I've got moves, baby." I jumped over the side of the truckbed and opened the passenger door. "Just you wait and see."

"**I**'ve got to go to the bathroom," I announced as soon as we pulled into Josh's driveway. I bolted out of the truck and ran to the front door. It was open, as usual, because Josh always said, 'If someone was willing to walk on my land and steal my things, they better be willing to die.'

I shut the bathroom door and twisted the little lock on the handle. I didn't have to pee, but that twenty-minute ride was long enough to sober me up. I was confident at Hattie's house, ready to jump on Josh and ride him until sunset. Now, I was terrified. I was so deep into my head, thinking about how bad Ashley was in bed, my leg shook.

Josh, of course, noticed, but I played it off like I was cold. Bad idea. He cranked up the heat. So, not only was I stressed and sweating from nerves, but I was also sweaty from the ride here. I lifted my arm and sniffed my pit. It wasn't bad, but there was a distinct deodorant smell. Not exactly sexy, if you asked me.

I grabbed the washcloth hanging on the rack and ran the corner under the water. I swiped the rag down my chest because salty boobs were nasty, then rinsed again and wiped under my arms. I looked in the mirror and straightened my high-rise, low-cut cowgirl dress, then decided to go to the bathroom now versus later, which was probably a good idea.

Of course, as I was sitting on the toilet, it dawned on me: *if my boobs are sweaty and gross...* I looked down at my freshly shaved vag and grimaced... *I bet that's sweaty, too.*

I finished, wiped, and then grabbed the washcloth again. I never worried about any of this with Ashley. Having sex with him was a once-every-few-months chore. If I was sweaty and gross, he never said anything. In fact, he never made any sounds. Our five-minute rides were awkward, silent, and unsatisfactory.

I slipped my panties off, then raised my leg to the toilet. No sooner did I wet the rag again and bring it to my center there was a knock at the door.

"You alright in there?"

"I'm fine!" I grabbed the towel hanging on the rack and dried myself, then tossed it and the wet washcloth beside the toilet. I whipped the door open and smiled. "Hey."

Josh smirked and gave me a once-over. "You're flushed. Is everything okay?"

Of course I was flushed. My rosacea flared up whenever I was nervous, excited, or angry, covering my cheeks and neck with a veil of crimson. Colson used to think it was funny to try and piss me off to see how red he could make me. Ashley never noticed my flare-ups, or if he did, he ignored them.

"I'm fine, just a little hot."

Josh's brows pushed together with worry. "Can I get you a glass of water or something?"

I stepped forward, swallowing the knot in my throat, and gripped his faux leather vest. The moment my hand touched him, something inside me burned to life. My body ached to be touched. If Josh knew how badly I wanted him, water would be the last thing he'd offer. "Or something."

I slammed my body into his and every thought and worry was gone when our lips met. Josh backed me into the wall and I broke our kiss, gasping for air. I barely registered the sting of my back hitting what might have been a door because Josh's mouth was on my neck again. He nipped and sucked, and I quivered, already on edge.

The door gave way as lips found my ear, and we were moving again. Josh pushed me on the bed. He tore that stupid cowboy vest off and pulled his shirt over his head. My eyes met his, silently begging for him to do something—anything.

He slid his hands up my leg, then smirked when he realized I ditched my panties in the bathroom. I bent my knees, my legs instinctually closing, but he pressed them open. "How bad do you want me, Layla?"

He dipped his head, running his nose along the inside of my thigh, nipping as he went. My hips bucked and he took that as an invitation to swipe his tongue along my center. I clawed at the sheets, desperate to get away, even though this felt amazing.

Josh held my legs and pulled me to him, keeping me there until I came undone. He lifted his head and then wiped his mouth with the back of his hands. "You taste delightful."

"Uh-huh," was all I could manage. My heart was racing. My legs were shaking, and I could feel my pulse in my eyelids. I stared at the ceiling and took a moment to catch my breath because that was amazing!

Josh's pants fell to the floor and I was hot again. I pushed onto my elbows and watched him adjust himself over his boxers while he stared at me, his eyes perusing my body.

"Tell me you don't want this now, Layla, because I make no promises that I'll be able to stop if you change your mind." He paused. Smirked. "Or how long I'll last."

"I'm ready. I want you," I admitted.

Josh dropped his boxers to his feet and sheathed himself with a condom, then pulled me by the legs to him. "You're beautiful, Layla, and you're mine now."

He kissed me, but our tongues moved out of sync because I couldn't focus on anything but the teasing pressure against my center. When I was at the edge of pissed and desperate, ready to tell Josh to make up his mind on if this was happening or not, he pushed inside me. I gasped and bit his shoulder to hold back my shock as he adjusted himself and then filled me completely.

He moved his hips, our bodies finding a rhythm that seemed meant for each other, and soon, the pressure between my legs morphed from uncomfortable to unbelievable. I arched my back, angling him to that sweet spot until I was riding a wave of euphoria. Eventually, Josh stilled, his body trembling as he finished.

"Wow." I closed my eyes, feeling my pulse thrum against my skin. "I think I understand why Amanda won't let you go."

I felt the bed shift and when I opened my eyes, Josh was beside me, the mess we made discarded. I rolled onto my side, still feeling the buzz beneath my skin, and smirked. "Too soon?"

"Never is too soon. Want to take a shower with me?"

I rolled over and kissed his lips. "Yes."

I SMILED, keeping my eyes closed a few seconds longer as Josh threaded his fingers through my hair, sending shivers of delight down my spine. I slept better last night than I had in years. Turned out multiple orgasms would do that to a girl.

"You are absolutely gorgeous," he muttered, then kissed my lips.

"Careful." I rolled into Josh's arms and gazed into his eyes. "You're gonna get me used to this."

His lips lifted in the corners. "Kinda hoping you do."

"I wish I didn't have to leave."

"So don't." He kissed my neck, finding that spot that made me shudder in delight. "Skip class tomorrow."

"I can't," I said as a war raged inside me. If I could, I would stay in this bed forever. We'd relive last night over and over again because that was hands down the best night of my life. But I liked my freedom, even if it came with stipulations. "My... um... midterms are this week. I need to study."

"If you weren't in school, I'd keep you hostage and never let you go." He slipped his hand between my thighs.

I spread my legs, welcoming his touch. "Pretty sure that's called kidnapping.".

Josh pressed against my center, but he didn't go in. I tilted my hips, anxious to feel him again, yet he purposely held back. "Or moving in."

"You want me to move in with you?"

Josh shifted his hand from between my legs and rested it on my hip. He looked me in the eyes and the intensity of his gaze made my stomach twist. "If we're still together next year and it doesn't mess up with your schooling, then yeah. I think I'd like to live with you."

Move in. I was worried about meeting his mom, but this took things to the next step. I weighed my options, knowing Josh was waiting for an answer, but there was a lot to consider.

We'd known each other for less than a year.

We'd only officially been dating for a week.

My parents would lose their minds when they found out.

But Josh was the sweetest man I knew. He never pressured me into doing anything I was uncomfortable with. He was respectful, had a steady job, and, if I was being honest with myself, I hated the drive from Orlando to the ranch.

"Well." I bit my lip, already knowing what my answer was. Dad always said there was no reward without risk. I thought Josh and I had something special. So...why not? "They have some online classes. I can talk to my guidance counselor about it."

"I'd like that." Josh chuckled as my stomach growled and

kissed the tip of my nose. "Come on. Let's get you some breakfast."

I sat up and pulled off the shirt I slept in. I was naked in Josh's bed again. From the look he gave me, breakfast could be on hold for a while. "After that, I should probably get on the road."

"Do you have to?"

He nibbled on my neck,and my eyes fluttered shut. "Maybe I can stay a little longer."

I decided to skip tomorrow's fundraiser. Aunt Tricia wasn't happy when I told her, but I wasn't on the schedule to work because I had taken the whole week off to prepare for my exams, including Saturday.

Since I didn't have to go in today, I decided to get up early, drive down to the farm, and surprise Josh. FaceTime helped curb the pain of being apart, but I missed him.

He came in through the kitchen's sliding door and froze as soon as he stepped inside. "Goddamn. That's a beautiful sight."

I finished straining the noodles, then walked around the kitchen island to kiss him hello. Josh was sweaty and smelled like grass and male musk, but he tasted like heaven.

"Are you hungry?" I turned away and headed to the stove. The roasted cherry tomatoes and ricotta were ready. I took them out, mixed them together, and then scooped the concoction over plated noodles.

"Starved." He took the stool across from me and dove in. I grabbed a beer from the fridge, twisted the cap off, and then handed it to him as he said, "This is delicious."

I smiled, pleased that the recipe I had seen online was a success, and sat beside him. "Grades were posted a little while ago. I got an A on my midterm in both my classes."

Josh nudged me with his elbow and grinned. "That's great, babe."

"Thanks."

He finished eating before I did and then started on the dishes. When I finished, I helped with the cleanup process by wiping down the counters and throwing away the trash. My parents never did anything together, let alone helped with mundane things. We had a chef, a maid, and, when I was younger, a nanny.

But cleaning up after a home-cooked meal as a team was nice. I could get used to it.

"We have two options for tonight." Josh closed the dishwasher and wiped his hands on a kitchen towel. "We can stay in and have a Netflix-and-chill kind of night, or we can go out to Sprocket Pond. It's usually a bunch of fun with a bonfire and whatnot."

"Well." I leaned against the counter and bit my lip. "I've never been to a bonfire, but I do like it being just you and me, too. Your call."

Josh hooked his finger through my belt loop and pulled me into him. "We've got all weekend together. Hattie will chew me a new one if she finds out you're here and I kept you to myself. Let's go to the bonfire. It should be fun."

I DIDN'T KNOW what to expect when Josh said we were going to Sprocket Pond.

An actual pond, maybe?

Nope, it was a large clearing with no grass, trees, or vegetation. Just a bunch of dirt with a huge muddy puddle in the middle of it.

Josh and I parked a few rows behind the circle of trucks surrounding the bonfire. The gang must have gotten here early because both Landon and Sam's trucks were in that circle.

Josh slipped his arm around my shoulder as we walked toward the fire. "You okay?"

I nodded, looking around, taking everything in.

Between the people on four-wheelers and the trucks riding through the mud, almost everyone was dirty. It wasn't chaotic like the mud festival Colson had taken me to. There, trenches were dug for people to drive through, and there wasn't a speck of dry dirt for miles. People drank and listened to music while riding around. It was fun.

Whereas this felt like we'd taken a party at Landon's house and moved it outside.

Sam sat on the roof of Landon's truck, his feet on the toolbox, and asked me the same thing. "What's wrong?"

"Nothing. It's just a little bit of culture shock. I've never seen anything like this."

Josh kissed my temple and squeezed my hip. "You'll be alright, I promise. Have a few beers and relax. It'll be a good time."

I climbed into the bed of Landon's truck and waved at the girl beside Sam. Every time I saw him he had a new chick on his arm. Sometimes, two in one night. He reminded me so much of Colson, it hurt.

My brother had dodged my calls all month. Sometimes, he let them ring until voicemail. Other times, the call was cut off with the F-you button after the first ring... you know, the ignore button. He never called me back, didn't return my text messages, and even blocked me on Facebook.

"This is Caymi," Sam said.

The girl beside him smiled brightly and extended her hand. I shook it but didn't commit her name to memory. Hattie poked her head out of the back-glass window and waved before disappearing into the cab.

"There's some people I want to say hi to. Do you want to come with me or hang here?" Josh as as he handed me a Mike's Hard Lemonade.

"I'll stay."

"Don't run off on me." He kissed my cheek and then disappeared into the crowd. I stayed with Sam, having idle conversations and listening to music.

When my drink ran out, I hopped off the truck and meandered through the swarm of people by the fire to look for Josh. We locked eyes at the same time. He waved me over and tossed an arm over my shoulder. "Guys, this is my girlfriend, Layla."

There were a few polite hellos and then the conversation continued like I had been there all along. I listened as Josh and his friends reminisced about high school and talked about how the town was changing—topics I couldn't contribute to.

The hours passed at a snail-slow rate. I followed Josh while he talked to more people than I could keep up with. When people I didn't know approached us, he introduced me. Even with the title of girlfriend being thrown around like money at a casino, a few girls still tried to slide between us and stake a claim to Josh. But he set them straight every time by telling those girls he was taken and crashing his lips against mine.

A few hours into the night, I was tired, but I didn't want to be a bother. I slipped out from beside Josh while he was talking to one of Bret's friends and headed for the truck.

I hadn't taken more than five steps before Josh took my hand. I turned and saw a puzzled face with glossy eyes staring at me. "Where are you going, babe?"

"I'm tired. I thought I'd lie down in the truck until you were ready to go."

"I'm ready. Just let me say goodbye to the crew. Want to come with me?"

I shook my head and took Josh's keys out of his pocket. "Tell them for me. I'm exhausted."

He smirked and leaned in, pressing his lips against my forehead before turning to his friends again.

The air was colder away from the fire. I crossed my arms

and zigzagged between haphazardly parked cars, focused until I heard a girl yell, "Hey!" from behind me.

I turned and looked over my shoulder as a woman I had never met drew nearer. She stopped about a foot away, fists on her hips, and asked, "You're Josh's girlfriend, right?"

"Yeah." I held my hand out, assuming she was another one of his friends.

But the woman spat at my feet and stuck her finger in my face. "You're a homewrecking slut!"

"Layla!" Josh shouted as he ran between the cars. He put himself between the woman and I, his eyes roaming over my body as if he were looking for injuries. "Are you okay?"

"Yeah... I'm fine."

He kissed my forehead and turned to the woman in question. "What the hell do you want, Kaitlin?"

"Nothing." Kaitlin held her hands up in mock surrender. "Just saying hello to your new girl." She wiggled her fingers at me and stretched her lips into a condescending smile as she backed away.

"Sure you are." He narrowed his eyes, watching Kaitlin until she was deep in the shadows.

"That was Amanda's sister," Josh said when we were in the safety of his truck. He cranked the heat up for a few minutes, letting me warm up, then turned the air down to a normal temperature.

"Oh. Okay. That makes sense then why she called me a homewrecker."

Amanda probably wasn't happy her speech didn't drive me off. In truth, it almost did. My life was complicated enough without adding in baby mama drama. Colson was ignoring me. My mother called me daily, trying to convince me that life with Ashley wasn't as bad as it seemed. My aunt was pressuring me to take on more responsibility. Dad acted like I didn't exist. And then there was school.

But I wanted what Josh described the other day—a love without limitations. A best friend, not a business partner—and there was only one person I wanted that kind of life with.

I knew I wasn't falling for Josh. Falling was a leap and then a smooth descent. I was tumbling down the mountain, feeling everything along the way.

Mom's house was filled with a mix of my brother's friends and mine. Thanksgiving and Christmas had always been huge, but tonight was more crowded than in years past because everyone was in town for the week. People I hadn't seen since high school had shown up, some with food, some with beer, and others just to hang out.

I smiled and nodded absentmindedly while staring at the patio door. I told Layla to park at the house and drive the Gator over. Everyone knew to leave the road clear, so they parked alongside it. Judging by how many people were here tonight, I'd say it was probably crazy out front, but she shouldn't have had any trouble getting to our home.

I took a sip of my soda and nodded again, agreeing with a conversation I hadn't heard. I'd been anxious all day, worried about Layla meeting Mom. I'd never brought a girl home, not specifically to meet her.

Sam's whistling pulled me out of my daze. He was such a tool, whistling at one girl with another in his arms. In my opinion, the girls who threw themselves at him were stupid. They thought they'd be the one to change his ways and then were scorned when he dropped them in a day or two. It was a never-ending cycle of disappointment and heartache, but Sam had attachment issues. I didn't see him letting anyone get close anytime soon.

I found the girl he had whistled at and grinned when I saw

her. Layla was walking onto the lanai, her arms clasped in front of her, with a beautiful yet timid smile.

I held my arms out and pulled Layla into a hug, lifting her off her feet. She smelled good—like strawberries and cream. She threw her head back, a laugh leaving her perfect lips as I set her back on her feet and cradled her face in my hands. I kissed her until my lungs burned and I was forced to take a breath. If I could, I'd never stop. I'd never let her go.

"You made it," I said, proud to have her there.

"I told you I would." She looked around, her gaze bouncing from one person to the next, taking in the two dozen people scattered about the patio. "This is a lot of people."

I dropped my arms and laced her fingers with mine. We walked away from the screen door and toward the beer pong table. "There's normally not this many, but Bret hasn't been home since August. Most of these guys are his friends."

"And yours." Layla waved, and Hattie left Kelly by the pool.

"Ahhh!" Hattie squealed. "I can't believe you're going to meet Sandy! She can't stop talking about you. I don't know who's more excited you're here tonight, me or her."

She pulled Layla into a hug and then reached for her hand.

"Oh no." I wrapped my arms around Layla's waist, refusing to lose her so early in the night. "She just got here. Go back to the friend *you* invited. I want some time with my girl."

Layla

"Oh, my heavens. Is this her?" the woman I assumed was Sandy —Josh's mom—asked.

She set the bowl of potato salad she was fixing on the counter and pulled me in for a hug. Both arms wrapped around me as she rocked me side to side. She set her hands on my shoulders and pushed me back a few inches. "Let me get a good look at you, sugar."

The woman was weary, with wrinkles around her eyes as deep as the smile lines on her cheeks. Her brown hair, the same shade as Josh's, though much longer, was pulled into a messy bun on her head and had streaks of grey throughout. "Mercy me, Josh. She's a beauty."

Josh slipped his arm around my waist, pulling me away from her. "Mom, quit. You'll scare her off."

"Oh, hush now, child. Darlin', I'm Sandy Thomas. Most kids around here call me Sandy," she said with a proud smile.

"Or Mrs. T. I call her Mama." Bret pulled me out of Josh's arms and twirled me once. "Remind me again, how did my brother score a fine piece like you?"

Sandy backhanded him across the chest and frowned. "Bret Allen, I taught you to talk to ladies with more respect than that."

I stifled my laugh by biting my bottom lip. These two were amazing—so warm and welcoming. My family would have judged Josh simply for being a country boy and turned their noses up at him. It was nice to see there was still kindness in the world. Josh, on the other hand, didn't seem amused and quickly pulled me back into the safety of his arms.

"It's a pleasure to meet you," I said.

"Look at that, Bret, she's got manners." Sandy fanned herself. "Lord help me, Josh, if you screw this one up, I'll tan your heiney."

Josh groaned and rolled his eyes. "Damn it, Mom! I'm not five. You can't say shit like that anymore."

"Watch your mouth around me, son." She picked up a spatula from the counter and waved it at him. Josh ducked behind me, hiding his face in my hair. "Now, Layla dear, after everything I've heard about you, I expect to see you around more often."

"It's all lies. I swear," I teased.

"Oh, hush now, darlin'. That boy couldn't tell a lie to save his life. He's real smitten with you."

"Mom!" Josh yelped.

"Well, it's true! Josh is my good boy." She reached out and took Josh's chin between her fingers, beaming. He rolled his eyes, and Sandy went back to stirring her potato salad. "Bret, on the other hand… that boy is gonna put me into an early grave."

"Aw, Ma. Don't say that. I'm not that bad," Bret insisted, swiping his finger in the bowl.

"Dagnabit, Bret! Out. Everybody out!" Sandy smacked his shoulder and then shooed us out of the kitchen. We had almost reached the back door when she yelled, "Oh, and don't use protection, dear. Y'all would make cute babies!"

"Oh, my God," Josh mumbled, shutting the door behind us. Once outside, he headed straight for the coolers and handed me a beer before taking one for himself. He downed half the bottle in one swallow before coming up for air. "Sorry about that."

I shook my head and set the drink on top of the cooler. He liked to drink around his family, and I didn't mind it, but I'd rather be clear-headed tonight. "I loved it. Your family is so kind, and mine… mine isn't."

Josh's phone sounded in his pocket. He frowned, looked at the message, typed a quick reply, and then put it away. "That was Amanda."

"Oh," I said, suddenly feeling out of place. Here Sandy was joking about babies and Josh had one looming on the horizon. Whether it was actually his or not was still up in the air. "Everything okay?"

"I want this to work between us, but it won't if there are secrets." He sauntered over to the cooler and took the beer I had rejected. He popped the tab and then took a sip. "She wants me to go to the ultrasound next week."

Something I didn't like tightened in my chest. This was the

kind of stuff that had kept me up at night. At some point, Josh was going to acknowledge that the baby could be his. If it was, he'd be a new dad, dealing with sleepless nights, doctor's visits, and diapers. And me? I'd either be pushed aside and forgotten or thrown feet first into stepmom mode. Neither sounded appealing. "Are you going?"

"No. I told her to piss off. That baby isn't mine."

I let out a breath, feeling the pressure in my chest decrease, but we weren't out of the woods. If my guesstimating was correct, Amanda was about five months. We still had four more until the paternity test results come out. "When's it due?"

"I don't know. Like I said, it's not mine." He drew in a sharp breath, exhaling slowly. "I've lost my appetite. You want to get out of here?"

"Won't your mom be mad?"

"Who cares? I want to spend time with you." He took my hand and pulled me into him. "Everyone else can piss off for all I care."

y guidance counselor, Miranda—who insisted I call her by her first name—typed away at her computer, unlocking the gates of heaven and hell.

Not really, but it felt that way because what she said would determine my future next semester. I was either on track with flying colors and staying in Florida for another six months, or I had gotten a C and my parents' money would dry up. In the latter case, I'd be stranded, left to fend for myself, disowned for breaking our deal, or forced to go back to Georgia and marry Ashley.

My leg shook.

I thought I had done well on my final exam yesterday, but grades hadn't been posted to the student portal yet and that last test was a beast. I second-guessed myself with every question.

Miranda stopped tapping the keyboard and spun in her chair to face me. She was a pretty woman in her mid-thirties with a pleasant personality. Most importantly, she was the only counselor on campus willing to see students face-to-face. All the others held their appointments either by phone or Zoom.

"Did you know your mother calls me every week?" I couldn't tell if she was irritated by my mom being a helicopter parent or simply sharing the information. Either way, the next time Mom and I talked we were going to have a chat about boundaries. "It's like clockwork. I know that every Wednesday at two-forty-five, she'll want an update on how you've assimilated into college life."

"I'm so sorry. My mother is…"

Miranda held up her hand. "It's okay. It's part of the reason I love being a freshman counselor."

"Oh, okay." I was sure Miranda assumed my mom was calling because she missed me.

This year was hardly different from any other, except instead of waiting at home for my parents to give me fifteen minutes of attention, I was in Florida, living my life. What was crazy was that I'd talked to my mother more in the last seven months than I had in my whole life.

No… Mom wasn't calling Miranda to check on me. She was snooping, looking for something to report to Ashley's father. She still had hope that our families would align and create a power team no one could mess with. They could align all they wanted, but it wouldn't be through me.

"You've exceeded my expectations this semester." Miranda turned her monitor so I could see the screen. I had ended with all As—a ninety-seven percent and a ninety-nine percent, to be exact.

I smiled, letting out the breath I had been holding, and relaxed in my seat. There was no room for arguing that I couldn't stay another semester. I had taken my C-average self and kicked ass. "Thank you."

"I was thinking we could up your workload to three classes." She slid a paper across the desk with my projected classes highlighted. "I know about your arrangement with your parents, but given how you excelled this semester, I don't see why you can't handle three courses."

I read over the list: Biology-1, lab, and geometry. It all looked great except for the lab option. That would require me to be on campus there was the pesky fact that all these classes were face-to-face. "I was thinking about trying some online classes next semester."

Miranda frowned and folded her hands over her lap. "Distance learning is tough. You have to be motivated because while the course has milestones, there's no one there to guide you. It's easy to fall behind. Are you sure you want to go this route?"

I slid the paper across the desk. "I can handle it."

Miranda's lips pulled tight, but she nodded. She might have been my advisor, but that was all she could do—give me advice.

Cutting hours of driving that could be used for studying out of my life made sense. Not devoting all my free time to a crappy-paying job also made sense.

Josh and I hadn't discussed how to handle bills, but we could figure that out once I got a job. Plus, my parents would still be sending me my stipend and I doubted Josh would make me pay eight hundred dollars a month in rent. "I'm sure."

"Well." Miranda turned back to her computer and tapped at the keyboard again. "I'm putting it out there that I don't recommend this option for you, but we can switch the core classes to virtual learning. You'll still have to come in for the lab, though."

"That's perfect."

My phone rang for the tenth time that day. I parked the Gator at the sliding glass door and stared at the screen, unsure if I should answer. It was probably Amanda, blowing up my phone for one thing or another. That girl had called and texted me nonstop.

Her belly hurt.

Her back hurt.

Her head hurt.

Her feet were swelling.

I gave up being nice. It did no good to tell her I didn't care. She still called. Still texted. So, I resorted to ignoring her. I hit the side button on my phone, darkening the screen but it rang again, seconds later. Whoever this was, they were on a mission.

"Hello?"

"Oh! You answered." Papers shuffled in the background as the woman cleared her throat. "Are you Joshua Thomas?"

"Who's asking?"

"My name is Clara and I'm calling from St. Mary's Hospital. How are you today, sir?"

I groaned and dropped my head against the headrest. This was baby-related. Of course, it was. "How can I help you?"

"I'm calling to discuss Bryson McGee."

I took my hat off and tossed it on the dash. This was low. Having the hospital call me. I knew I needed to get the paternity test out of the way, but come on. "Listen, Miss—"

The woman blurted her next sentence in one breath, simultaneously stealing the air from my lungs. "Amanda McGee passed during childbirth."

If I had been standing, I would have fallen to my knees. I didn't like the girl, but I didn't hate her, and I'd never wished for something like this to happen.

"She's been calling me," I blurted, words and reality not connecting. "She can't be dead."

"That was probably her family. You're listed on the forms from her doctor as the father. I need you to come in and sign some papers."

"I..." It wasn't mine. The baby wasn't mine. I said that sentence more times than I could count but now that he was born without a mother, I didn't feel as confident. "I'm not the father."

"Oh." The woman audibly sighed. "That's unfortunate. Are you sure?"

"We were going to do a paternity test to be certain, but yeah." My stomach fell. As much as I didn't want to be the father, I couldn't imagine growing up without a family. All that kid had now was Amanda's crazy sister. Their dad was in jail for selling meth and their mom had been in and out of rehab for as long as I had known the girl. It was a shitty situation.

"How soon can you get here? Paternity tests take, on average, three to five days for the results to come back. Bryson is in the neonatal unit and will be for a few weeks, but there's paperwork that needs to be signed. Child Protective Services has to get involved if you're not the father, and then things get messier."

I pulled the key from the ignition and shoved it in my pocket. Mom needed to know what was going on. I had kept the baby thing a secret, but with Amanda out of the picture this changed things. If the kid was mine there wouldn't be any shared custody agreements or visitation. Everything would fall on me—the bills, the doctors, the late nights, all of it.

"Um." I looked at the time on my phone and sighed. This was a lot to take in. I still didn't think the boy was mine, but I needed to get my ducks in a row. Just in case. "I can be there in about thirty minutes."

"Okay." Her rolling chair slid across the floor. "Perfect. I'm running to the NICU so we can get the paperwork ready. For the kid's sake, I hope he's yours."

"Thanks, I think." I didn't know how I felt about this kid. I didn't want him to be mine, but I didn't want him lost in the system either.

I hung up and texted Mom, telling her I was picking her up in five minutes. She didn't ask questions; she just said okay. I loved that about her. Whenever I needed something, she was there, no questions asked, ready to help.

I opened the sliding glass door to the house and stopped in my tracks. Layla was pouring two glasses of wine in the kitchen, smiling as she held one out to me. I shut the door and took the glass but set it on the counter. She wasn't supposed to be in town until tomorrow night.

Normally, I'd be stoked she was here early, but I didn't have the time to entertain her tonight. I needed to get to the hospital, talk to Mom, and figure out how to pay for this kid's hospital bills.

I hoped he wasn't mine.

Convincing myself there was no chance I made the kid when he wasn't here was one thing. Now that he was born and breathing, needing support from I didn't know how many machines, it made that point one percent more real.

Scarier.

"What are you doing here?"

Layla set her glass on the counter and wrapped her arms

around my waist. "I finished work early and took tomorrow off. I thought I'd surprise you."

I took Layla's wrists and peeled her off of me. I didn't want to be touched. I wanted to be alone to process that Amanda was... God. She was dead. How the hell was she dead? "You shouldn't have come. I don't have time for you right now."

Crap. That came out wrong, but it wasn't a lie. I looked at my phone. Five minutes had passed. Mom was probably waiting by the road, wondering where I was.

Layla took a step back and crossed her arms. "I'm sorry. What?"

I groaned and ran my hand through my hair. "I need to go somewhere, but you can't come with me and I don't know when I'll be back."

Layla stared at me, brows bunched together in confusion. It frustrated me because every second I wasted was one more added to the d-date where I found out my future. My hands shook with nervous energy. I wasn't ready to be a dad.

"Are you kidding me?" Her arms dropped to her sides, and she took a step back.

I was running out of patience, but I was trying. It wasn't Layla's fault I had to go, but I really needed to leave. "Seriously, Layla, I'm trying my hardest not to be a jerk right now, but I'm running out of time. I have to go but you seem like you've got something on your mind. I can spare five more minutes. What is it?"

"I thought I'd surprise you with good news. I gave up my lease, but if I'd known you would become such a jerk I wouldn't have."

I ran my hands through my hair and looked up at the ceiling. "What did you do that for?"

My phone dinged in my pocket. I didn't need to look to know it was Mom probably wondering where I was and if I was okay.

"We talked about this." Layla took my hand in hers. It was small and warm, and I couldn't help but think about the baby and how tiny his hands must be. "I'm taking next semester's classes online so I can be here. With you."

I pulled back and grabbed my keys off the counter. I couldn't do this right now. "Are you serious, Layla? We talked about next year, not next month."

"January is next year."

"Well, it doesn't work for me right now. Get your apartment back." I stalked to my room and grabbed a clean shirt. Mine was sweat-soaked and stank.

Layla followed me down the hallway to the bathroom and watched me put on my deodorant. She waited for me to face her before saying, "I can't. They've already got a new tenant lined up."

I set my hand on her hip and slipped past, heading for the front door. "Then get a new place because you can't live here. Not right now."

Layla chased after me and grabbed my arm, stopping me from getting into the truck. "Why are you being like this?"

I gripped the door until my palm hurt. "Because I didn't ask you to rearrange your life for me!"

"Josh." She sucked in an audible breath. "I..."

"Layla." I frowned, not meaning to hurt her feelings. "If you're still here when I get back, we can talk. But I have to go. Don't wait up."

Mom took my hand and squeezed it. I told her everything, minus the particulars of how the baby was made. She had made a good point. Amanda had said she was on birth control, but she could have lied and she had supplied the condom. That girl had been hell-bent on us being together; she could have poked holes in it.

If that was the case, there was a good chance this baby was mine.

"Everything will be okay," Mom insisted, but I had a sinking feeling that my life was about to change.

From the moment that woman at the hospital had called me, I felt it—this blanket of dread. Walking under the yellow lights of the hospital hallway, that blanket grew heavier with each step. I took a breath, unable to fill my lungs, and then attempted to let it out.

"How can I help you?" the triage nurse asked.

The room spun. I could barely keep myself upright, let alone answer the question. I gripped the counter and sucked in another ragged breath.

"We're here for a paternity test," Mom answered for me.

"Oh!" The nurse perked up. "Baby McGee. I've been waiting for you. Can I see a photo ID?" She read over my name, matching it to the one on her paper. "That little guy is a trooper." She told the other nurse at the counter she'd be back and buzzed us through the doors. "Do you want to see him?"

"I… uh…" No. No, I didn't. Seeing Bryson would make him that much more real. Right now, he was a dark cloud looming over my future. But seeing him, hearing him cry… nope. No, thank you.

"We'd love to." Mom smiled up at me with hopeful eyes. I nodded, feeling that invisible blanket wrapping itself into a noose.

The NICU wasn't what I had expected. Babies weren't in clear bassinets, waiting to be adored like in the movies. Most were in covered boxes, unable to be seen. Rows and rows of those boxes with monitors and machines attached filled the room. It was scary.

"Here he is." The nurse stopped in front of one of the few clear boxes without a cover.

Looking at Bryson, something in my heart squeezed. Wires stuck out from his chest and arms; there were tubes in his nose, and another going down his throat. The scariest was the IV. It stuck out of the little guy's head, taped to a scraggly mass of dark hair.

"What's wrong with him?" I touched the box, knowing without a doubt the kid was mine. He looked like I had when I was born—half the size, but just like me.

"He's doing better than most babies his age, but he needs help breathing because his lungs aren't fully formed yet, and he doesn't have the coordination to eat independently." The nurse grabbed a cover and placed it over his cubicle. "I was hoping you'd want to see him, so I was ready. Babies this young like to be in the dark. They grow better that way."

"Like they're in the womb."

The nurse nodded and smiled. "Exactly."

"We appreciate being able to see him." Mom squeezed my arm. Tears pooled in her eyes and I could tell she was thinking the same thing I was. We'd still do the paternity test, but Bryson was mine.

Amanda had been right all along.

I followed the nurse to her vampire station in a daze. In less than five minutes, my blood was drawn and we were free to go. Mom stopped at Bryson's box again. I needed a better word for the thing he slept in. *Box* reminded me of a coffin and the last thing I wanted was for him to end up like Amanda.

My throat burned, growing tighter with each swallow. I left Mom with Bryson and hightailed it to the truck. Every instinct told me to run, but I forced myself to walk and maintain my composure. I smiled and nodded at the nurse near the door.

Left foot.

Right foot.

One after the other at a painfully slow pace.

I made it to the cab of my truck, shut myself inside, and stared at the concrete wall of the parking garage in front of me —space number twenty-eight.

That was how long Bryson had cooked in Amanda's belly.

Twenty-eight weeks.

I beat my fists against the steering wheel, not caring that the horn blared a few times. He was too young to know this kind of suffering. Not able to breathe on his own. Unable to eat. It wasn't fair.

He hadn't asked to be brought into this world, but here he was, the underdog, already fighting to make it.

I rested my head against my hands and gave in to the sobs taking over. My fingers gripped the steering wheel until my skin hurt. I needed pain. Pain I could control.

My passenger door opened and Mom wrapped her arms around me. She pulled me into her and I couldn't hold back anymore. I cried like my newborn should have been doing but he couldn't because of all those damn tubes.

"Shhh." Mom rubbed her hand in circles on my back, like she had when I was a kid. "Everything is going to be all right."

I sat up and looked her in the eyes. Hers were bloodshot,

like mine, from fallen tears. It choked me up even more because Mom was the strongest woman I knew.

"Will it? He's so tiny, Mom. How can a baby be that small and survive?"

"Hey." Mom cradled my cheeks and wiped my tears with her thumbs. "Bryson has the best doctors available. Besides, he's a Thomas—even if his name doesn't reflect it yet—and we are survivors. That boy is going to be fine. You wait and see."

She kissed my forehead and then patted my leg. "We should get home. There's nothing more we can do tonight and Layla is probably worried sick."

Layla. Shit. I had forgotten all about her in the wake of things. I pulled my phone out of my pocket, knowing good and well that I had screwed up tonight. I just hoped it wasn't too late to fix things.

Me: Hey. Mom and I are headed back to the house. Are you still home?

I set the phone on the dash and left the hospital. It was a forty-minute drive from the hospital to the farm if I went the speed limit. Mom and I had made it here in twenty, but she had shot me more than one look about how fast I had been driving. This time, I slowed down to only ten MPH over the limit. About halfway through the ride home, I checked my phone at a stoplight, but Layla hadn't responded. So I texted her again.

Me: I'm sorry about earlier. We should have that conversation again.

Layla: You said plenty the first time. I got your message loud and clear.

"Honey, the light is green."

I tossed my phone back on the dash and continued down the road. I waited for it to ding again, but the sound never came. As I pulled into the driveway to drop Mom off, it was clear that Layla wasn't at my house anymore. All the lights were off and even though it was too dark to see the driveway, I could tell her car wasn't there.

"This might be a stupid question, but are you okay?" Mom asked, and I knew she would sit in the passenger seat until I answered. She was a patient woman, but when she asked a question she expected an answer.

"I screwed things up with Layla tonight." I dropped my head against the rest, feeling that burn welling in my eyes again. Today had been too much, first the baby and now Layla. I needed life to cut me a break.

"Sweetie." Mom touched my arm. I forced a smile because I knew it would make her feel better, but I was dying inside. "Layla will understand. Today was... well, it was unexpected."

"Yeah. I hope so."

Mom smiled and headed into her house. I followed the drive to mine, unsurprised when it was empty. I picked up my phone and called Layla. It rang and rang before going to voicemail. I hung up and called again, this time only getting one ring before being ignored. That pit in my stomach expanded into a black hole, sucking me in.

"Layla, it's Josh. I fucked up earlier and I'm sorry. I was going through some shit, still am, but I'm getting a handle on it. Call me back."

I hung up and called Hattie. I hoped Layla was there and didn't drive back to Orlando. It rang twice before she answered. "Hello, handsome. What's up?"

"Is Layla with you?" My pulse ravaged my chest. I needed her to be there. I knew I said I wanted to be alone earlier, but I changed my mind. I wanted to hold Layla, tell her how I was falling for her, and fill her in on everything. Hopefully, she'd understand and stick around. If not, I didn't know what I'd do.

"No. Is everything okay?"

I exhaled, feeling my whole body shake. News about Amanda and Bryson was going to spread like wildfire. I was surprised it hadn't gotten out yet. If there was any chance for Layla and me to make this work, she needed to hear what was going on from me. That was if I could get her to answer the phone. I leaned the seat of my truck back, too beat to go into the house. Today had been a nightmare and I had a feeling things were only going to get worse.

"I don't know."

Chapter 37

The paternity test came back. Bryson was my kid.

Bryson was still in the hospital.

The nurses said he would be there for a while, but I had hoped to have him home for Christmas. Every day he stayed, the bills grew. I didn't have insurance. Amanda had Medicaid, but I wasn't sure how it all worked since she passed. The woman from Child Protective Services told me not to worry and that everything would work out, but I knew better.

Doctors had co-pays.

Hospitals had stupid, expensive co-pays.

I was looking at thousands of dollars I didn't have, all to support a baby I wasn't prepared for. I couldn't even work overtime because the ranch made money by selling cows and I had only one calf born this year.

On top of it all, Layla was still ignoring me. Her apartment had been cleaned out and rented to someone new, and no one would give me her forwarding address—not even her aunt, who made it more than clear she didn't appreciate me showing up at her office unannounced.

I sagged onto my worn leather couch and attempted to watch something on TV, but nothing held my attention. I was dog-tired from working the ranch and checking on Bryson, but my mind wouldn't give me a minute's peace.

Every time I closed my eyes, I saw her face. Her heart

breaking over and over again. I didn't know if my memories were becoming clearer as time passed or if my mind started filling in the blanks with new micro-details about how that day went down, but it sucked.

As for my nightmares, they were so intense I couldn't sleep unless I blacked out.

Every breath hurt. Every movement, even something as simple as getting out of bed in the morning, was a struggle. The guilt of how I treated Amanda before she died ate me alive. Worrying about Bryson chipped away at my soul, and any part of me that was still kicking drowned wondering about Layla and what could have been if I hadn't been such a jerk. The only thing that helped numb the suckiness that had become my life was whiskey.

I grabbed a half-empty bottle off the end table and brought it to my lips. I had them everywhere. Not on purpose—they just seemed to show up. Beside the toilet. In my bed. Under the table. It was like I had a whiskey fairy leaving me gifts until I finally gave in to temptation at the end of the night.

I took a swallow of the amber liquid, then chased it down with another and another until the pain in my chest didn't hurt quite as much. Eventually, my eyes grew heavy. I closed them, hoping I would drift off into a dark hole of nothingness and not another nightmare about Layla moving on, but my sleep was interrupted by a banging.

I groaned and opened my eyes. There was only one person I wanted to see, and she didn't knock—let alone bang. No. She would waltz in and make herself at home because that's what this place was supposed to be. Her home.

Until I fucked it up.

"Dude." Landon gave me a once-over and frowned. I took a sip from the bottle the whiskey fairy had placed in my hand and his lips turned down further. "You look like shit."

"Tell me something I don't know." I turned, leaving the door behind me open, and fell back onto the couch. I closed my eyes, knowing Landon was silently judging me for the overflowing trash, leftover takeout containers, and dirty dishes.

"Where the hell have you been, man?" He slid a basket of laundry out of the recliner and took its place.

He waited for me to respond. I waited for him to leave. One of us was going to lose. Chances were it would be me because I could only sit with my eyes closed for so long before Layla crossed my mind. I didn't want to think about her, so I opened them and took another sip. "Busy."

He grabbed a sock from the basket, balled it up, and threw it at me. "Too busy for your friends?"

Too busy. Too tired. Too everything.

I didn't have the energy to laugh and pretend the world was all sunshine and rainbows. I had a kid whose bilirubin wouldn't level out and had been under blue lights for weeks, so I couldn't touch him. A farmhand who was pissed because my head wasn't in the game anymore. An overbearing mother who said she was worried about me. And a girlfriend who wouldn't call me back.

Ex-girlfriend.

"Josh!"

"What?" I yelled, losing all control for the millionth time that day. I didn't have highs anymore, just lows and reds. Reds that made me yell and lose my temper for no apparent reason. "What do you want from me, Landon?"

Landon took my attitude in stride. He didn't raise his voice or even a hand at me. He crossed his arms, eyes narrowing into slits. "I want to know what's happening, but this..." He gestured to the disaster that was me and my home. "This isn't you, man."

"I don't know where to start." I lifted the bottle to my lips again, but it was empty. "I could start by saying that Amanda is dead. She bled out or something. It's all fuzzy to me, but she's dead."

"Sure, that sucks, but I thought you didn't like the woman."

"That's beside the point." My hands shook. I hadn't told anyone besides Mom what was going on. Maybe that was why I was so strung out. I needed someone in my corner to remind me that I had this and everything would be okay. Mom was great, but that was her job—to tell me what I wanted to hear. "I found out the kid was mine the night I lost Layla. She kept pressuring me into a conversation I wasn't ready to have and I snapped. I said things I couldn't take back and now she's gone."

Landon was quiet for a beat. He leaned forward onto his elbows and sighed. "Tell me how I can help."

"I don't know." I dropped my face into my hands because that was the million-dollar question: How could anyone help?

Amanda's sister met me at the NICU and repeatedly told me how grateful she was that I had stepped up. She said she wasn't ready to be a mother, but she told me to say the word and she'd help me however she could.

But what could you do for a baby stuck in a plastic box with wires sticking out of him?

How could you teach him how to eat so he didn't need a feeding tube anymore?

You couldn't. I couldn't do anything but sit back and watch. Waiting for either good news or bad. Every day, I drove to the hospital and prepared myself for the worst. I had seen babies who seemed fine take a turn and nearly die in a split second.

Families were crushed and sometimes ripped apart. Nurses were yelled at for not doing enough when, in reality, they lived and breathed these babies.

"Tell you what." Landon slapped his hands on his thighs and then stood. "Hattie's birthday is in a few weeks. Let's turn the party into a Chuggies for Huggies."

"You don't have to do that."

Landon grabbed the empty whiskey bottle from my hand and another from the end table. He walked to the kitchen, tossed them in the trash, then looked around. "It's no biggie, man. People come and drink on my dime half the time, anyway. At least they'll be doing something good for a change."

He smirked and grabbed the Chinese takeout boxes I should have tossed last week. "As for Layla, I've got a plan."

Present Day

I didn't know why I was coming back. I mean, I missed Josh. I missed him more than I could even begin to explain, but I didn't want to see him.

Not for one minute.

I put myself out there for him in December. I was willing to risk losing my family to be with him because I believed in us. And what did Josh do?

He shut me out.

Pushed me away.

Did he try to call and take back what he had said? Of course. But he hadn't just broken my heart—he broken my trust. I couldn't believe when he said he would do something and what was a relationship without trust?

So, even though it killed me, I didn't listen to the voicemails. I didn't return the text messages. I stopped looking at the pictures. And I locked everything that had to do with us in a box and threw away the key.

The only reason I agreed to come back to this godforsaken town was because Hattie insisted that Josh hadn't been coming around. Every day got easier, but I didn't know if I could keep my resolve if I saw his face again.

"You have no idea how much I've missed you. Two months was just too long." Hattie squeezed me tight when I walked inside. It felt so good to be back. Like a piece of me that had been missing had finally been found.

Landon found us a little while later on the couch and hugged me too. It was a little strange because we weren't affectionate, but it made me feel missed. I liked it. "Hey, pretty girl, long time no see."

I smiled, more nervous than excited, but I tried to focus on the moment. I was here with my friends. Celebrating Hattie's birthday.

Tonight was going to be just what I needed. A good time with good people, enough alcohol to push my feelings away, and... diapers?

I pointed to the mini mountain of diapers stacked on the kitchen table and frowned. "Um... is there something you haven't told me?"

Hattie laughed and threw her arm over my shoulder. "Yes, but now isn't the time."

Two months.

Two months had passed since I last saw Layla and my life had spiraled into one big clusterfuck since she walked out the door. I had six cows die this week. They found some lantana and by the time I realized what happened, it was too late. That was roughly thirty thousand dollars gone.

And then there was Bryson. He was officially a Thomas with official insurance, which required a minimum five-thousand-dollar co-pay for everything that had been done so far. The hospital offered a payment plan, but that was still a lot of money I didn't have and medical bankruptcy wasn't an option.

On the bright side, if everything went well this weekend Bryson would be discharged on Monday.

I was terrified.

He was just shy of four pounds and too tiny to fit in normal preemie clothes. He needed special diapers, expensive formula, and pacifiers—all of which I could handle—but I was used to the annoying beep of his heart monitor. What would happen if his lungs weren't as strong as we thought and he stopped breathing?

What if he rolled over in his sleep and choked himself?

I wasn't worried about screwing up. No new parent knew what they were doing. They winged every decision and hoped for the best. I was petrified of the unknown, of the anomalies that were preemie babies, things I didn't know how to prepare for.

Maybe that was why I was sitting in my truck at a party I'd inadvertently hijacked, struggling to break the seal on a bottle of Jack Daniels.

That and I was about to see Layla again.

A twisting feeling settled in the pit of my stomach, so I chased it away with a shot. The liquid burned as it went down, but it was a familiar burn. One I'd gotten too used to over the past two months. When I no longer felt the worry-knot, I put the cap back on the bottle.

It was now or never.

I slipped around the backside of the house, careful not to draw any attention to myself. I wanted to find Layla and watch her for a few minutes to see if she was on the defense or having a good time. Her mood would directly affect how the night was going to go.

I found her on the back patio next to Hattie, beautiful as ever. I was so transfixed by her that I didn't see the trash can to my left. I bumped into it and muttered under my breath while trying to keep it upright so beer cans wouldn't spill everywhere and blow my cover.

Layla's brows pushed together as her gaze moved from Hattie to me. What was left of her smile fell from her face. She dropped her drink and ran into the house.

Every cell in my body screamed at me to chase after her, and I didn't think I could have stopped my feet from following her even if I wanted to. My heart pounded in my ears when I reached the bathroom door she hid behind. Hattie must have left the bedroom unlocked in case something like this happened.

"Layla." I set my palm on the door, too nervous to pound on it lest I scare her or piss her off. I was walking on thin ice as it was. I didn't need anything else stacking up against me that night. "We need to talk."

The door ripped open and I almost fell forward from the sudden change in balance. Wet trails of mascara ran down Layla's cheeks. If life hadn't gutted me before, it had now. I had taken this beautiful, strong woman and broke her. Even if it was an accident, her pain was my fault.

Layla's face pinched together, her sadness morphing into something darker. She balled her fist and punched me in the stomach.

It didn't hurt, but I pretended it did and doubled over. It was a jerk move, but I played the sympathy card. What could I say? I was buzzed and needed to break the ice between us somehow. If faking that she'd hurt me was the way to go, then so be it. I groaned, covering my stomach.

"I'm sorry!" Layla threw her arms around me and cried into my shoulder. She grabbed my shirt like she was scared I'd disappear and whispered, "I'm so confused. I don't know how to feel right now."

I wrapped my arms around her. She smelled amazing, like warm summer nights and bonfire smoke. "Trust me. I get it. Most days, I'm a mess. Yelling at everyone. Shutting myself in a dark room. I even ate a pint of Rocky Road ice cream, and I'm lactose intolerant."

Layla giggled and I smiled for the first time in weeks. This felt right, her and me, but I needed to get everything out in the open. The longer I waited, the more I risked someone else spilling the beans about Bryson. "Baby, I—"

Layla jolted back. Her hands pressed against my chest as she shoved me away. "No. You don't get to call me baby. You don't have that right anymore."

My jaw ticked. A burn rose in my throat that I choked down. I refused to let her see the tears on the brink of escaping. I needed to support her, make her realize how sorry I was, and not be a blubbering fool who needed comforting. Even if that was all I wanted—to be in her arms again.

Layla sat on the toilet lid with her face buried in her hands. I closed the door and knelt in front of her, desperate for forgiveness but at a loss for words.

What was there to say to someone whose heart you'd shattered?

Especially when I knew her pain. I lived with it every day.

She sniffled, wiping her nose on the back of her hand. "What happened between us? One minute, everything was great, and the next, it all blew up in my face."

I sat back on my feet. This was my chance to lay it all on the line. The opening I needed to explain myself, but I couldn't find the words.

"I hate you." My voice was barely above a whisper, but I knew he heard me. My words bit into him like a viper, the sting they left written on his face, and I wished I could take them back because they were a lie.

I didn't hate Josh. I might've loved him and that was the problem. He didn't know, which was another problem, and he could never know.

Ever.

He could never know how much he had hurt me. How often I cried myself to sleep. How every single night I fought with myself not to return his calls or read his messages.

"Baby," he said so quietly, I almost missed it.

Baby.

That word cut more than he knew. It cut through the walls, the pain, and the tears. That single word made me want to try again, to find comfort in his arms.

His eyes looked up at me, pleading. There was so much pain and sorrow in them. I felt myself caving, giving in to the heartache. I wanted to forgive Josh for the way he talked to me, but then I thought about my dad and how he treated Mom . There were so many secrets and lies in their lives that a spider wouldn't know how to walk on that web.

All I could remember about the night I left was thinking that this was how it started. If I let Josh's actions slide like they were no big deal, he would do it again. Each letdown would be worse than the last, each secret more detrimental than the one before.

I hadn't escaped a loveless marriage with Ashley just to end up in a relationship with a duplicitous jerk.

I walked past Josh, without waiting for him to fabricate an excuse to cover the truth, and headed toward the kitchen. A wave of nausea hit me. I paused in the shadow of the doorway for a moment to catch my breath and force my nerves back down.

I did it.

I stood my ground.

Kneeling on the bathroom floor, I watched Layla walk out of my life.

Again.

My stomach contracted so violently that I barely had time to lift the toilet seat. Remnants of a burrito and most of the whiskey I drank earlier splattered inside the porcelain bowl. I heaved again, then once more, until my stomach was empty.

I wiped my mouth with the back of my hand and then washed them in the sink. Glancing in the mirror, I looked like shit. The bags under my eyes were as dark as night and my skin was a ghostly white compared to the sun-kissed tan it usually was.

I took a deep breath and followed Layla into the house, prepared to chase after her, but she was gone. I ran my hands through my hair and looked around one more time. I felt it bubbling up again, that red fire I couldn't control. The fire that made me say stupid things to the people I cared about. Without thinking, I punched the wall nearest me. The skin on my knuckles split, red and raw, but I could clench and unclench my fist, so at least it wasn't broken.

"What the hell, Josh?" Hattie stared at me wide-eyed.

I didn't have an answer for her. I couldn't tell her that I had screwed up again. I didn't even know what I had done wrong this time. I stormed past her and ran to my truck. There were only a few secluded places in town that Layla knew about. I hoped she'd go to one of them and not drive back to wherever she emerged from.

I drove around for hours, hitting all the spots we went to together. I went to the places that screamed Layla. All the beach access points. The Red Onion. The mall. The art museum. Riverside. The pier. I hit every place I could think of between Fellsmere and Vero.

I was filling up at the gas station, wracking my brain for where else she could be, when my phone rang. I pulled it out of my pocket so fast I almost dropped it. It was Layla. I didn't know whether to be excited or worried.

"Hello?" I waited, but she didn't respond, so I said hello again.

"Hey. So..." She sighed, and my stomach flipped. "I ran out of gas. Can you come get me?"

"Of course!" I hung the nozzle back on the holster. If I were a good guy, I'd run inside the gas station and buy a gas jug to take fuel to Layla.

But I wasn't a good guy.

I was greedy and tired and I missed her. If I screwed this up, I might not get another chance. "Where are you?"

"Um." There was another pause.

My body trembled again. I wanted another drink to settle my nerves. It was too easy to drown everything out, but I wanted to feel it all tonight.

The fear.

The excitement.

And, hopefully, find some kind of happiness again.

Finally, she said, "US1 and MLK Boulevard."

I didn't hesitate. I was in my truck, barreling down the highway before I finished telling her, "I'm on my way."

L ayla stepped out of her rental car and crossed her arms as I pulled up beside her. She wouldn't make eye contact with me, but that was okay. I didn't need her to look at me. I just needed her.

"Your knight in shining armor is here to save the day."

That earned me a smile and a sigh. "I'm sorry I ran out on you. I didn't think it through. Once I got in my car, I realized I didn't have any place to go. I'm staying with Hattie, but I couldn't go back in there. So I drove, and drove, and well…" She shrugged.

"Believe me when I say there have been plenty of times I wanted to run away."

"But that's what makes you stronger than me. You don't." Her gaze fell to her feet and a tear slipped down her cheek.

I stepped forward and pulled Layla by the arm into me. I held her tight, taking in the moment because I didn't know if this would be the last time she'd let me. Layla might have been upset about us, but she was a strong-willed woman. No matter how much it hurt, if she thought being apart was for the best, she wouldn't come back to me.

"I'm not strong." I smoothed her hair and kissed the top of her head. "I'm an asshole who doesn't know how to handle stress. I blow up at the people I care about and push them away."

"Like you did with me." It wasn't a question, but she was right. I sabotaged us by not realizing what I was saying.

I couldn't wait to fix things. The truth was my only shot at winning her back, so I laid everything out there, starting with the catalyst that ruined us. "Amanda died giving birth to Bryson."

Layla reared back and looked up at me, her mouth slack. She reached up and cupped my cheeks, searching for the answers to a question she had yet to ask.

"I found out right before you came over. It threw me for a loop because that meant I needed to step up." I swallowed hard, feeling the familiar burn of tears in my throat. I cleared it away, but the pressure moved behind my eyes. "He's my kid. I don't know how, but he is."

I felt the first tear fall, but with her I wasn't ashamed to show how hard life had been. Layla wiped it away with her fingers. She pushed onto her toes and pressed her lips to mine. It wasn't a long kiss, but it was what I needed to regain control.

She smiled up at me, her fingers lacing behind my neck. "You're going to be a great father."

My lips twitched and lifted at the corners. "Do you want to see him?"

That pretty smile fell. She stepped back and looked around for someone to save her. "I... I don't know. Won't he be asleep?"

I shrugged. "I'm not sure. I've never been to the hospital this late."

The fear on her face transformed into worry. She crossed her arms over her chest, a red flush creeping up her neck. I had missed how easy it was to read her. Red on her neck meant she was upset—either worried or nervous. On her cheeks, she was embarrassed or happy. If it was on her ears, she was angry.

"Is he okay?"

I took her hand and opened the passenger door of my truck. She got in, which made my heart soar. We either had a shot at fixing things between us, or she was curious about

Bryson. Either way, it was more time we got to spend together. I'd take it.

I closed her door and ran over to my side of the truck. I needed to get the beast in gear and down the road before she changed her mind. "Yeah. Premature babies need more time to grow. We had to wait until Bryson could do everything a full-term baby could." I grinned, feeling excited for the first time about my situation, and glanced at Layla. "But I finally get to take him home on Monday."

"That's great, Josh." She laced her fingers with mine and, for a moment, things felt like they used to.

I knew I had a lot of work to do to get us there again, but this was a start.

en itty-bitty fingers curled around one of mine. Bryson was wrapped in a blue teddy bear blanket with a matching baby beanie, and he was the tiniest thing I'd ever seen.

Even so, he was beautiful. He had Josh's hair and his nose, but the eyes and lips were all Amanda—the perfect combination for this little heartbreaker.

Bryson looked up at me and smiled. I knew it was involuntary. Babies that little didn't know what they were doing yet, but I couldn't help but beam down at him.

The nurses said he was the quietest baby they'd had in a long time. He almost never cried, which, to me, would have been terrifying, but they assured me he was a happy little guy. I had to trust them because this was their job, but his quietness still worried me. I didn't say anything because he wasn't my baby, and I didn't want to worry Josh over nothing. He had enough on his plate.

After a few minutes of holding perfection, I handed Bryson to Josh. He took him in his arms and offered a bottle, which the little guy greedily guzzled. I watched them interact, awestruck at how sexy Josh was as a dad. I knew there was a chance I'd run into him this weekend, just like I knew I'd be at war with myself over our breakup. But I didn't know I'd fall even more in love with him than when I left.

I never would have guessed that one.

I pulled my phone out of my pocket and glanced through the forty-five unread text messages he had sent. There were hints about Bryson but nothing that outright stated what Josh had been dealing with.

I felt bad. Had I known what was going on, I would have come back and tried harder to understand what he had been going through that night. Instead, I had shut him out like a child throwing a fit.

"You're great at that, feeding him."

He beamed at me, then looked at his son again. "We've only been on the bottle a week, but the little guy knew exactly what to do as soon as I put the nipple in his mouth."

"Just like his daddy." I flushed, not meaning to have said those words out loud.

I sat back in the cushioned seat behind Bryson's clear bassinet and looked around. Dozens of baby beds filled the room, each hooked to its own set of monitors and devices. I couldn't help but wonder if Bryson had been like them a few weeks ago or think about how traumatizing the experience of becoming a dad must have been.

Josh shifted Bryson over his shoulder and patted his back. When he burped, Josh placed him in the bassinet and patted his back again until he fell asleep. The nurse on duty beamed, nodding approvingly at Josh's daddy skills.

I bit my tongue and pushed back a rage I'd never felt before. Jealousy wasn't something I wrestled with often, but watching that girl give him googly eyes pissed me off. I linked my hand with his as we walked past her and out of the NICU, just in case the woman needed a reminder that this daddy was off-limits.

"You're good at that."

Josh pulled me into him and wrapped his arms around me. "What?"

"Being a daddy." I slipped my hand into his back pocket, a move I had seen in a Netflix rom-com—only in the movie, it had been the guy's hand in the girl's pocket. It worked. Josh looked down at me, a playful grin on his face.

When we reached the parking garage, Josh opened the passenger door for me. "It's pretty late. We should probably get your car. It's not in the best part of town."

I got in and waited for him to take his place on the driver's side. My heart was racing. I was nervous to make the first move between us, but in reality, I was just responding to the million moves Josh had made to try and get me here. I only hoped I wasn't too late. "Do you think I could come back to your house tonight?"

His lips twitched and I could tell he was fighting a grin. "Of course. Mi casa es su casa."

My stomach twisted. Had we both not overreacted back in December, his home could have been my home.

Josh must have felt the same heaviness I was wrestling with because he lifted the center console and pulled me closer. I leaned against him, closing my eyes as he kissed my crown.

It wouldn't be easy, but we still had a shot.

That is, if he still wanted me.

I wasn't sure when I fell asleep, but it must have been on the ride to my car because I had no memory of crawling into Josh's bed. I peeled the covers back and walked to the window, and the morning light momentarily blinded me. When my pupils adjusted, I peeked through the curtains. Just as I had suspected, my car wasn't in the driveway.

I stretched my arms up, noticing but not caring that my jeans from the night before were lying on the floor. Either I kicked them off in my sleep, or Josh had pulled them off because he knew how I felt about sleeping with pants on.

He knocked on the door and waited for me to say, "Come in," before stepping inside. "I thought you might be hungry." He set a tray with orange juice and an onion bagel with cream cheese on the dresser.

"You remembered." My cheeks heated against my will, which caused Josh's lips to lift at the corners. I missed his smile.

Mom told me I must have been having too much fun in Florida because my laugh lines were deeper. I smiled on purpose because I refused to limit my emotions for the sake of beauty.

He sat on the edge of the bed, his gleeful grin faltering as he shrugged. "Is it lame to say I ate your favorite breakfast daily because I missed you?" He didn't give me a chance to answer before shaking his head and adding, "Never mind. I don't want to know."

"Josh." I exhaled a heavy breath and then sat beside him.

This was the conversation I had run from the night before at Hattie's house. I didn't know what to say because I didn't know what I wanted. My heart told me to give him another chance, that our problems stemmed from a stupid misunderstanding, but my head had told me to be cautious. But then, after seeing him at the hospital with Bryson last night, I didn't know what I wanted anymore.

"Don't." Josh fell onto the bed and stared up at the ceiling. His eyes were puffy and bloodshot, his cheeks blotchy and red. "Don't say goodbye. If you're going to leave, just do it."

"Josh," I whispered, taking his hand in mine. "I have to leave, but that doesn't mean I want to."

His silence hurt more than anything he could have said. All he'd done since I left was beg me to come back. In a way, he already said everything he wanted. It was my turn now.

"I love you," I whispered, and the admission made the room spin. I'd never said those words out loud, not even to my parents. Josh was the only person in my life to earn them. If he didn't feel the same, I didn't know what I would do.

That got his attention. He turned his head toward me but still didn't say anything. My heart raced, but I pushed through the anxiety because if I didn't get these words out now, I never would.

"If you still want me, I'm willing to give us a shot again, but it won't be easy. I'm living with Colson in Georgia because I lost my apartment. My parents have no idea. If they found out, they'd cut me off, so flying back and forth isn't an option. I'm willing to do whatever it takes, though, if you are."

"Layla." Josh pushed onto one arm and cupped my cheek with his other hand. "All I've wanted was another chance with you. I don't care how hard it is. I'm in."

"Really?"

"Yeah." He kissed me and pulled me onto him. I straddled

his lap, my fingers curling at the base of his neck while his hands ran down my sides. He flipped us to where I was lying down and he was on top. "I love you too."

Tears welled in my eyes. I was relieved, elated, and terrified all at once. So far, I wasn't a fan of love. It hurt more than I ever thought possible but it was also the best thing I had ever felt in my life.

"You do?"

"That's a stupid question. Of course, I do."

"Alright, on the count of three, you're going to read each other's sign," our photographer, Chelle, said, waiting for us to write something on a dry-erase board. I knew exactly what to say.

We were supposed to be shooting Bryson's first birthday pictures for his party next month. We'd already taken the cute solo shots and the family ones. All that was left was the cake smash.

At least, that's what Josh thought.

This past year had been insane. Josh and I spent the first four months of our relationship long-distance. We saw each other one weekend a month and the whole week of spring break.

It was horrible.

I missed him so much it hurt. I missed Bryson, too, and almost every milestone—holding his head up, pushing onto his arms, sitting on his own, babbling. Every FaceTime call left me feeling hollow and lonely.

So, when Josh officially asked me to move in with him at the end of the semester back in May, I couldn't refuse. My bags were packed and I was on the first plane after finals.

Colson hated the idea but let me go anyway. What was the worst he could do? Tell Mom and Dad? I did that myself after I was settled and had a part-time job at the Red Onion.

Dad was pissed, insisting I was making a huge mistake and

warning me not to come crawling back when everything fell apart. Mom, on the other hand, said she was proud of me for forging my own future and agreed to keep paying for my college.

They would come around. It might take some time, but I had a feeling they'd get over themselves before next summer.

Why?

Let's just say I called Chelle with some big news and an even bigger request. She squealed and said she had the perfect plan, which was why Josh and I were back to back, with Bryson playing with some Legos on a blanket in front of us.

I capped my marker and took a breath. I was so nervous I could puke, but that would ruin the photos. And my dress.

"Ready! One..."

I could do this.

"Two..."

Even if Josh had been working later than usual on the farm this week, everything would be fine. Bryson's bills were paid. He was healthy and hitting every developmental milestone. I was acing my classes and had a steady job. This would be great.

"Three!"

Here went nothing.

Josh and I turned around at the same time to read each other's messages. I didn't read his. Instead, I watched as his face morphed from happy to shocked to excited. He dropped his board and cupped my cheeks, pulling me into him.

"You're pregnant?"

I nodded, happy tears running down my cheeks. I didn't realize I had skipped a period until Hattie started complaining that she was always on the rag for the holidays—every holiday, whether she was due or not. I laughed, then realized I couldn't remember when my last period was.

I pulled up the tracking app on my phone, and it yelled at me in big red letters that I was twenty days overdue. The pee-on-a-stick test I took said it could take five minutes to get results, but it had only taken thirty seconds before blinking the word "pregnant."

Josh's grin stretched wider and he dropped down on one knee.

My heart skipped a beat and I felt like I couldn't breathe. I glanced down at his board, which had fallen to our feet, face up.

"Want to be a family?" it read.

I looked back at Josh and the ring reflecting off the sun in the little velvet box. It was a single diamond set in yellow gold. Beautiful. Classic.

"Well?" Chelle called out.

"Oh!" I was so stunned I'd forgotten Josh asked the question. "Yes! My gosh, yes!"

Josh stood and wrapped both arms around my waist. He spun me around in a circle, then crashed his lips against mine until we were both breathless.

"This was my grandmother's ring." He pulled the diamond out of its box and slipped it onto my finger. "I know girls like white gold these days, but I wanted you to have something that meant something to me, not just a store-bought nothing."

"It's perfect." I rested my head against his chest and smiled at the camera. "Just like us."

The End

LOOKING FOR SOMETHING ELSE TO READ?

Sign up for my newsletter to access an exclusive, subscriber-only section of my website. There are freebies, bonus chapters, and more!

JOIN MY NEWSLETTER

FOR WEEKLY UPDATES ON ALL THINGS BOOKS AND BAILEY PLUS RECEIVE AN EXCLUSIVE SHOP DISCOUNT

And turn the page to learn about some other great books Bailey has to offer.

Looking for some love in your life? Bailey's contemporary romances range from sweet to spicy, with everything in between.

Enemies to Lovers, High School Bully, Athlete Antihero, First Love, Girl Next Door, Completed Duet

Book 1 in the Broken Love Series

Piper

Most people don't think about the day they'll die. They coast through life, blissfully unaware of how their time is ticking away. I wasn't like most people. I welcomed death, wanted her to take me away from the prison I called life, but she refused. I tried twice only to survive. And then, when I thought I had nothing left it came. A reason to live. Rex was a small, unexpected ray of light my world of darkness that blossomed into a beam of sunshine. I thought, maybe this was why Death didn't take me. Maybe she knew that if I held on a little longer things would turn around. But the third time Death came to my door wasn't by choice. Someone else brought her, and I fear this time she might take me.

Rex

Being the son of a country star sucks. My parents are never around, I move every year or so, and I have no real friends. Everyone around me has an agenda. Everyone except Piper Lovelace. I can't get that girl to notice me. Trust me I've tried.Thankfully, fate stepped in and gave me the break I needed. I've got her attention, now I need her to give me a chance.

Enemies to Lovers, High School Bully, Athlete Antihero, First Love, Girl Next Door, Completed Duet

Book 2 in the Broken Love Series

She's beautiful. Fierce. Nothing at all like the girl I used to know, which is absolutely terrifying because Danika Winters is the only person outside of that room who knows the truth. She could ruin me, and I'm not talking about my reputation. I couldn't give two shits about what the kids at St. A's think. I'm talking major, life-altering, jail time ruined. I'll do whatever it takes to keep her quiet. Even if it means destroying the only person I've ever cared about.

**Fall In love with a
Bailey Black Book Here**

Frienemies to lovers, Fake dating, High school romance, Love triangle

Asher Anderson is a dick.

We aren't friends, so when he seeks me out in the cafeteria on the worst day of my life, I'm suspicious. When he tells Liam Heiter that we're dating, which couldn't be farther from the truth, I want to kill him...Until I see Liam's reaction.

Liam—my best friend, the guy who crushed every hope of us *officially* being together—is jealous. He has never looked at me this way and I love it.

So, I play along. Maybe watching me with someone else will make Liam suffer like I have the past four years. And maybe, just maybe, he'll come to his senses and realize we belong together. It's not like I actually *like* Asher. At best, I tolerate him. What's the worst that can happen?

**Fall In love with a
Bailey Black Book Here**

Small town, Opposites attract, Cowboy, New girl in town,
Unexpected parenthood (+denial)

Josh

I met the girl of my dreams in a church parking lot while my
best friend was having sex in my truck. Her name was Layla
and she was trying her hardest to ignore me and them from two
parking spaces over. I swear, I've never seen someone so
beautiful in my life. I've also never struggled to get the girl
but,for some reason, my foot and my mouth became friends
that night in the worst of ways.

Cheesy pickup line, that failed? Check.
Inability to form coherent sentences? Check.
Ego crushing letdown? Yup. That happened, too.

I can't put my finger on it, but there's something about Layla
that sucks me in. I need to get to know her. Spend time with
her. Make her mine. Who knows, maybe she will be the one to
finally settle me down. That is, if I can convince her to give me
the time of day.

Layla

Everything about Joshua Thomas screams, run away. His sharp jaw. Those vibrant eyes. Lush lips that have probably tasted every girl in this tiny town. I know better than to give him a chance, but knowing what I should do and listening are two different things. He makes my heart flutter in ways I thought only possible in Hallmark movies. He makes my legs shake from one look. I resisted him once. I don't know if I can do it again.

**Fall In love with a
Bailey Black Book Here**

Second chance, The dare/bet, Insta chemistry, Learning to love, Shared Pasts

I've sworn off men forever! Okay, not forever, but for a few months. After my last hook-up, my vag needs a reset because the last man to touch me broke it in the worst of ways. Not a problem until my new dance partner comes into the picture. He's turning into my forbidden fruit, tempting me in ways I didn't know possible.

I have three months of celibacy ahead of me and eight weeks to whip my new dance partner into shape.

Someone save me.

SCAN TO READ A
SAMPLE

Fake dating, Second chance, Friends to lovers, Everybody can see it, Short and Spicy novella

A wedding. A lie. And regret.

I'm in over my head with not one but two ex-boyfriends at the same wedding. Both of which I haven't seen in over a year. When the one who ripped my heart into pieces backs me into a corner, I grab the other and kiss him.

Yup. This is how I ended up fake dating Noah Ruckers, and let me tell you, it's an emotional roller coaster. I thought I'd put my feelings for him behind me. We spent years as friends after our break up, nothing more. But no matter how hard I try I can't forget what his lips feel like. Or the way his arms wrap around me.

In two days, I'm walking away. There is no future for us. But that doesn't mean I can't pretend.

**Fall In love with a
Bailey Black Book Here**

Fake dating, Second chance, Friends to lovers, Everybody can see it, Short and Spicy novella

Holly Flynn is a leprechaun who grants wishes—but with a dangerous twist. Each wish comes at a price: once it's fulfilled, the "victim" forgets everything before their wish—and her.

When a gorgeous stranger asks for one unforgettable night, things take an unexpected twist. The chemistry between them is electric, and soon, Holly's struck by a terrifying thought: She doesn't want him to forget her.

Then, a week later, he knocks on her door. And he remembers everything.

Why does he remember, when no one else does? Is it fate—or is her magic betraying her?

**Fall In love with a
Bailey Black Book Here**

How About a Fantasy Adventure?

Dive into the completed Neverland Novels. Characters have been aged up for this darker, grittier version. If you like your fairytale retellings with hot, ruthless, morally gray love interests, you'll enjoy this series. The Lost Darling is the first book in the main storyline. Please read this series in order.

Twisted Fairy Tale, Peter Pan Retelling, Multiple Love Interests, Morally Gray Males, She's Mine, Scorching hot lost boys, Spice, and more!

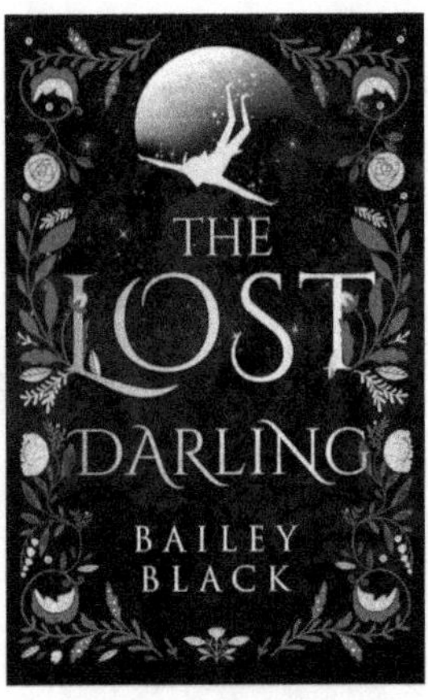

Second star to the left and continue until morning.

I got that line tattooed on my wrist the day I turned twenty-one. So much symbolism in such a simple sentence. At the time, it was a nod to the future and the infinite possibilities to come, while reminding me to remember the past and to look for magic in the world.

Growing up, nothing was ever what it seemed. The shift of leaves on a tree was a faery skipping by. Shooting stars were a chance to make wishes. Shadows were souls stuck between this world and the next, mirroring a life they once had.

My imagination was limitless, the world a wonderful adventure waiting to unfold.

It's easy to lose that sense of wonder with the weight of life on your shoulders and I wanted a reminder to get me through the hard days.

Most importantly, it was an ode to the boy who earned the title of my first crush, even if he was animated. Peter Pan wasn't a *save the damsel* kind of prince. He was daring, and selfless, and took care of the ones he loved. He was a friend to all but never afraid to fight the Pirates when their moral compass broke. Wendy was an idiot for leaving him. She rushed home to a heartless world full of men willing to lie through their teeth to get down her pants.

But that's the beauty of a book, the characters are perfectly flawed. Damaged just enough that we still love them. Whereas reality is nothing but empty promises and baggage the size of mountains.

The day I got my tattoo, I would have given anything to be whisked away into a fairytale. My world was crumbling, and all I wanted was to go back to when life was simpler. I didn't realize I had sealed my fate in ink.

Branded myself as one of the Lost.

Neverland was everything the stories made it out to be. Beautiful. Full of magic. Filled with handsome men and debonair pirates. But the author of my favorite tale left out one crucial detail.

In order to get there, you have to die.

**Fall In love with a
Bailey Black Book Here**

Looking for Something Else to Read?

**Fall In love with a
Bailey Black Book Here**

A witch in a world where magic is illegal, A revenge mission, A rescue mission, Death. People die. Sorry, not sorry, 2 love interests (not a RH and not a triangle), A touch of enemies to lovers. He falls first she falls harder

I had a plan. Find the soldier who killed my family and make him pay. It should have been an easy feat. I'd done it over a dozen times, taking out each member of that regiment one by one, but the mission went sideways. It all started with the man in the woods. The one my webs of magic couldn't sense even when he stood before me. Then my partner made a mistake, and now he's lying in one of the Crown's dungeons, fighting for his life. I couldn't leave him to die, but I couldn't just walk into the castle either.

Or maybe I could.

With the help of some unexpected allies, I entered the Culling—a one-in-a-lifetime chance to become queen. I have no interest in winning the prince's heart, or the crown. My only goal is to get into the castle, find my friend, and get out before someone realizes I'm a Cerise.

But when the welcome ball turns from a grand event into a

nightmarish dance of death, all eyes are on me. As if that's not bad enough, the soldier, the one who took my family, he's here.

If you loved "The Selection" by Kiera Cass and "From Blood and Ash" by Jennifer L. Armentrout, get ready to fall in love with this enchanting fantasy romance!

Fall In love with a Bailey Black Book Here

To me, this is the hardest part of the book to write because there are so many wonderful people who help make each story come alive and every time I get to this page, my mind goes blank.

First and foremost, I want to thank my BFF Alexandria James, who put her debut novel on the back burner to beta read/edit/help me not loose my sanity through out this process. Without her picking my brain and helping me to organize my thoughts, this book would still be sitting in my massive pile of incomplete projects. (Shameless plug...her amazing vampire paranormal romance is available in May!)

A special thank you to Elizabeth Murphy for being my star beta reader. I would be lost without your attention to detail and your suggestions.

My editors Beth at Magnolia Author Services and Lily at Partners in Crime Book Services, you ladies rock. Your attention to detail has this book polished and shining.

A huge thank you to my Mom for reading everything I write, even if it makes me cringe when she gets to the dirty bits.

To my husband who likes to give me grief when I spend too much time typing but gets on my case when I haven't touched my computer for a week...I love you.

To the bloggers and bookstagrammers who bring my stories to the world. You are amazing! I cannot begin to express how grateful to you I am.

To everyone I'm sure to have forgotten because I'm Dory's second cousin twice removed and feel like I'd forget my head if it wasn't attached.

Finally, I'd like to thank my readers. Every time you open one of my books, you make my dream come true.

Thank you.

Xoxo

Bailey B.

ABOUT THE AUTHOR

Bailey B is an up and coming New Adult author. She lives in Lehigh Acres Florida with her husband, twin girls, and two fur babies. She enjoys (but doesn't get to take part in because of her crazy daughters) the simple things like Disney+ binge watching, Netflix romcoms, reading and sleeping. She reads two to three books a week and thinks if narwhal's are real animals then unicorns might be too.

www.ingramcontent.com/pod-product-compliance
Lightning Source LLC
Chambersburg PA
CBHW070418310726
48977CB00003B/746